Lost in the darkness; exposed by the light.

Looking back over his shoulder, Mikael could see a line of pale Shahi, almost ghostly in the dim light of their lamps, staring at them as they went. The Shahi's faces were carefully blank, as if they didn't want to show their judgement. Mikael could read it, though: the fear, the uncertainty, the nervousness. Apparently they had some experience with bonded pairs, if what Mandric and Tai said were true, but it must not have been a good experience.

The line of Shahi surrounded the edge of the low platform they were finally led to, watching as if to make sure that Mikael would stay as far away as possible. Mik supposed it could be worse, since the platform at least wasn't a hole in the ground, and wooden floorboards were warmer than the cold ground ever was.

"Can they go away now?" Mikael muttered to Mandric as they settled in their bedrolls. "It's—"

"Creepy," Katjin supplied, curling up against Mikael's back. He yawned. "I don't think I'll sleep a..."

And then Katjin snored.

Mikael rolled his eyes at Soren, who cracked a grin. "If you ignore them, they might go away," Soren pointed out, fluffing up his own small pillow and rearranging the blankets to his liking.

As if they understood Soren's words, the Shahi faded into the trees that shrouded the dark pathways of the hirhai.

"Sleep, lad," Mandric said softly, setting up his own bedroll on the other side of Soren. "We'll deal with it in the morning."

Mikael swallowed. That's what he was afraid of.

GLBT YA Books from Prizm

Banshee by Hayden Thorne
Changing Jamie by Dakota Chase
City/Country by Nicky Gray
Comfort Me by Louis Flint Ceci
Heart Sense by KL Richardsson
Heart Song by KL Richardsson
I Kiss Girls by Gina Harris
Icarus in Flight by Hayden Thorne
Masks: Evolution by Hayden Thorne
Masks: Rise of Heroes by Hayden Thorne
Staged Life by Lija O'Brien
The Suicide Year by Lena Prodan
The Tenth Man by Tamara Sheehan
The Water Seekers by Michelle Rode

KL Richardsson

Heart Song
KL Richardsson

Illustrations by Pluto

Prizm Books
a subsidiary of Torquere Press, Inc.

Heart Song

This is a work of fiction. Names, characters, places, and incidents either are the product of the author's imagination or are used fictitiously. Any resemblance to actual events, locales, organizations, or persons, living or dead, is entirely coincidental and beyond the intent of either the author or the publisher.

Heart Song
PRIZM
An imprint of Torquere Press, Inc.
PO Box 2545
Round Rock, TX 78680
Copyright 2008 © by KL Richardsson
Cover illustration by Pluto
Published with permission
ISBN: 978-1-60370-552-3, 1-60370-552-X
www.prizmbooks.com
www.torquerepress.com

All rights reserved, which includes the right to reproduce this book or portions thereof in any form whatsoever except as provided by the U.S. Copyright Law. For information address Torquere Press. Inc., PO Box 2545, Round Rock, TX 78680.
First Prizm Printing: December 2008
Printed in the USA

If you purchased this book without a cover, you should be aware the this book is stolen property. It was reported as "unsold and destroyed" to the publisher, and neither the author nor the publisher has received any payment for this "stripped book".

He read to me, he believed in me, and when I told him what I wanted my fairy tale to be, he didn't laugh.

For Dad. It's not a boat, but it is a small thank you.

In memory of Lynda, who gave me a voice and a story to tell.

Heart Song
KL Richardsson

Illustrations by Pluto

Heart Song

Chapter One

Hoofbeats thundered around him, echoing in his ears until it was all he could hear. They reverberated off each other until Mikael couldn't tell where the horses and their riders were coming from. All he could do was press his face into Katjin's back and hope that Shanti could outrun the cavalry. Shanti was an amazing horse, one of the best the Clan had ever bred. The cavalry, though, also rode some of the finest Clan horses, and that could be a problem.

So Mikael tried to imagine himself as light as a bird, tried not to breathe, and let Shanti carry them away to safety.

Around the storm of hoofs, he could hear the rush of blood roaring. He squeezed Katjin tighter and tighter, trying to do *something*. His body demanded that he act, that he act *now*, but he wasn't sure what he could do. It wasn't like he could get off Shanti's back and push her any faster.

He hated riding. He hated horses. He hated being chased. He hated the thought of the cavalry, that they'd kidnap him again and attempt to—attempt to— He shuddered. He wasn't going to think about that now, not when they were almost free.

"Why didn't you bring another horse?" Mikael wheezed into Katjin's ear. "Silly to risk Shanti like that…"

"Why didn't you wait for me to rescue you?" Katjin yelled back into the wind. His grip on Mik's arms tightened.

"Can't leave you to have all the fun," was all Mikael could get out. Katjin's responding snort lightened his mood a little bit.

This wasn't exactly what he'd had in mind, when he'd sung the aiding song at Katjin all those moons ago. Then again, the life of a renegade 'path wasn't exactly one he would've chosen either…

Once there was, in days long gone, a land of three peoples who hated and warred with each other for generations. The Horse Clans raided, the Highlandfolk brooded in their hills, and the Lowland farmers and fisherfolk cowered in fear. That's the way it was told to every Lowland child from the time they were small.

No one remembered exactly what it was like when the Clans rode down from their high plains and ravaged the cities of the Lowlands. That was over five hundred years ago, even though the Empire liked to make you think it was yesterday. Most of the soft-bodied Cityfolk, especially the ones who lived on the coast, had no idea what the small villages experienced, hearing the strange howls in the night as tens and hundreds of horse-bound men and women rode down and burned everything in sight. As far as Mikael knew, not even the Clanfolk could tell you exactly why they started the pillaging and burning in the first place. From what he'd seen, they had some of the best pasture-lands in the Empire–especially considering the thin, rocky soil he'd grown up on.

Lightbringer was the traditional title of the Emperor or Empress, honoring the history of the ruling house and all they had done to instigate peace. The Empire brought light to a dark land and a darker age. That's what his tutor had told Mikael when he was small. That's what the Empire used its 'paths to enforce: gratitude toward the savior power, a sense of security that it would never happen again as long as the Empire and its 'paths were in control. Yes, there had been no war in two generations. Yes, most people could ride from one end of the Empire to the other, completely unmolested by bandits or other dangerous folk.

From what Mikael had gathered over the years, listening to Father's business conversations and reading into the gossip and complaints of his older sisters, not everyone was convinced of the Empire's benevolence. Not everyone enjoyed the thought of a 'path rummaging through their mind or their heart at a whim, and not everyone wanted the protections the Empire offered. Three races had been brought together into an odd sort of marriage under Empire law, and all three clashed with each other at plenty of opportunities. There was peace, but it was begrudging peace, and time would only tell how long that peace would reign.

When the light came to take him out of that dark, dank cell, it hadn't been the Empire who did it. They—whoever they had been, since the only voices he'd recognized in his feverish state had been Father's and the seneschal's—had thrown him into the literal darkness, imprisoning him for the stars only knew how long. Mikael's memories past his thirteenth birthday were fuzzy at best, confused and feverish at most. There was no one left to tell him exactly how long he'd been in delirium after his empathy first kicked in, and how much longer yet he'd been locked in that dark cellar at the country house, all but forgotten.

There was only so much pounding on the walls you could do 'til your hands cracked and bled. You could only scrabble at the stone for so long until your fingers swelled, the skin scraped off. Even then, though, the pain eventually left you alone in the dark, 'til there was nothing left but the black and the silence and the double-edged sword of peace that the darkness brought with it. He had been alone, aye, but there were times when that had been a blessing in disguise.

That dark cell had been a relief, when he wanted to be honest about it. The stone walls had insulated and protected him from the assault of emotion and noise and *loud* that had been so confusing in those last days. He'd used the dark and the quiet as his shield to pull himself back together—and to try and not lose himself in the process.

That was the story of growing up though: Father's denial, Mother's avoidance. His sisters had treated him normally enough, with the teasing and the torturing and being kids, he guessed. He'd been so much younger than the three of them, and while Mother and Father had seemed to spoil him terribly, it had always been at a distance, almost as if they wanted to give him his way just to keep him out of theirs. He had been a convenient child, only called in when the situation demanded, when Father needed to trot out his perfect son before visiting Merchant's Guild members, or parade him quickly through the streets of town to prove he existed. His three sisters had run wild with the other children in town and at the country house, merchant- and lower-class alike. Mikael had always been kept inside, with the occasional tutor to make sure his reading, writing, and figuring were up to standard. The rest of the time, he'd been alone with his horse or practicing with his sword. All because of his wrist. All because of the fact that he wasn't marked.

His sisters had whispered once about a brother, born even before the oldest of them, taken away by the Empire within days of his birth. While his father had never talked openly about hating the Empire, there'd still been the occasional dropped hint, the occasional angry word that Mikael caught—even before his empathy manifested. Father had always watched him so carefully from afar, constantly drilling his tutors about his talent for learning, any innate gifts for swordsplay or otherwise. There had even been talk of finding one of the legendary fencing instructors that came out of the Highlands every so often; no one had seen one of them in generations.

So his sisters played and enjoyed and laughed, while Mikael studied the sword and the parrying dagger—since he was still too light to carry a shield—and the rises and falls of the marketplace. He helped Father cipher on occasion, he helped Mother log what sold and what didn't each season, though that was almost the only contact he had with her. Toward his tenth year, Father finally took him to the occasional meeting with the traders who provided the specialty goods, just to see how Mikael did at judging people and their motives. Apparently, he did it all too well, because Father soon put an end to that, especially when some of the merchants began to ask why Father's only son wore gloves all the time, hiding whatever brand he wore on his wrist. It was common practice, when you met someone for the first time, that you bared your wrist to show if you were 'path or not.

Mikael never did this, though. His unmarked wrists were illegal in the Empire, and he could never figure out why his parents dared almost flaunt that fact. Why his parents had never sent him away, he didn't know, almost as if they were tempting their own fate. That was probably the question that haunted him most: why would his parents risk their lives—and the lives of his sisters and everyone in the household—like that? What power games were they trying to play? The Empire would have caught them—and him—eventually. They always did. He couldn't exactly ask them now, though. Sometimes he hoped he wouldn't have the chance to ask them, just because he was afraid of what the answer might be. That was where the old rumors came into play, of an older son who might have been stolen by the Empire, and how his father refused to give up another child. Except that sheer stubbornness most likely only brought doom upon the whole family.

He started fainting, until his sisters teased him about being as fragile and delicate as one of those noble ladies that occasionally came to Stoneridge. Any gatherings or parties would overwhelm him until he blacked out, and then even those rare walks down the main street of Stoneridge, just a middling-sized Lowlands village, became too much. Mother fretted from across the room and Father worried, never actually doing anything about it, and then they hid him away. It'd be impossible to guess how long that was, since there was no telling how long his fever had lasted, and how long his parents waited before sticking him in that dark room.

And when the door opened, blinding him momentarily

in that flash of white light, he'd fled faster than he knew possible. He'd known he'd only get one chance. His father wouldn't have risked letting him out unless there was a reason, and Mikael had his doubts that the Empire would let a renegade 'path, especially an unmarked one, escape with no retribution. The light had burned so bad that he stumbled, not even able to see anything even if he had looked back as he fled the only home he had known. He couldn't count the number of times that he fell, though he was sure that his too-soft feet and battered shins could have told him. Instinct had told him to run, and he did. Straight into the arms of a slightly-clueless, utterly brave and impossibly stubborn Clansman singing the aiding song.

Stars bless, but he'd almost cried when he heard that aiding song. It was probably the most wonderful thing he'd ever heard in his life, followed closely by Shanti's hoofbeats as Mikael had fled the Empire camp just weeks ago, trailing an entire squadron and 'paths behind him.

The Empire was no lightbringer. For him, that role belonged to one person alone: Katjin.

They'd made their daring escape and Katjin's cousin, Soren, had ridden to their rescue with a troop of armed Highlandfolk at his heels. Mandric, de facto leader of that group of Highlandfolk, had proposed taking the three of them over the mountain to the Shahi, because the Shahi could best deal with Katjin and Mikael's... situation. While the decision hadn't really sat well with either of them, they'd decided to do it. The Shahi couldn't all be the demons that the Empire had painted them to be. Mandric was an exceptional person, and according to popular belief, he was supposed to be a crazy recluse who did questionable things to his sheep, just because he was Highlandfolk. It made Mikael wonder exactly how much the Empire had been toying with Lowland thought and for how long, since he obviously wasn't the only one who suspected this.

So they went up and over the mountain, daring narrow, rocky paths that just barely clung to the mountain face as they wound their way through the passes. They went up so high that it burned when they breathed, and the dry air seemed to suck all the moisture out of Mikael's lungs. They came down into a damp, humid bed of greenery and poor Katjin almost had a heart attack. None of the stories whispered about the Shahi mentioned that they lived in trees. Clanfolk have a mortal fear of trees. Maybe it was too much time spent on their open plains. Katjin explained it once as the feeling of being caged, being hemmed in on all sides until you can't even look *up*, because even the sky has been taken from you. For people who lived surrounded by empty sky and grasslands, Mikael could understand why they might take such fear to heart. If you were used to open and space and nothing but air to keep you in, having such giant trees looming over you would probably be more than disconcerting.

Maybe that's why he'd loved the plains at first. There'd been no sign of that heavy darkness that had kept him in for all those countless days and moons. All he had to do was throw open the tent flap, and there was the sky, arching endlessly overhead. But after a while, the openness had gotten to him until he felt lost and small and alone. It wasn't the same solitude as the darkness, but the light could still be just as frightful. At least in the darkness, you could hide. In the light, in the openness of the plains, everything was exposed.

Oh, the trees. Towering giants draped in green, protecting from sun and rain and any other inclement weather. Granted, your safety and security depended on how well you could cling to a branch hundreds of lengths above the forest floor, but you were still so high above everything that it was magnificent. He'd played for hours in the woods around the country house when he was a child. These huge trees reminded him of that, reminded him of simpler times and peace.

Maybe it was the insulating power of wood, rather than the reverberations that seemed to happen when surrounded by stone. Maybe it was the fact that everyone in the Shahi village seemed to be shielded in some way, even though this was the largest number of people he'd been around in years. Maybe it was just the weight of the trees and the sense of immense age of the forest, like his little firefly life didn't matter so much in the great span. Not even the Empire mattered that much, when you considered the circling of stars and moons and everything like that.

It was peace. Mikael had found peace. He wasn't sure if he ever wanted to leave.

There were obstacles, of course. There were problems and issues that hindered his plans even before he mentioned them to anyone else. The first was his bond to Katjin—they still couldn't stay separated for more than a short period of time without feeling like they were going to throw up. The headache, Mikael could ignore, but the nausea was what got him every time. It didn't help, either, that Katjin's pain reflected back, adding to his own. Soren called it a continual cycle of pain, but only 'til Katjin threatened to blood-bind Soren to the two of them so Soren could experience the joys, too. That shut Soren up.

The second obstacle, stemming from his bond to Kat, was the fact that the trees literally scared Katjin shitless. Mikael knew how close his poor Katjin came to losing everything in his bowels the moment they ascended up the tree trunks in that little Shahi basket. Soren, brave cousin as he was, put on his bravest face, but even the mighty Horse Clan warrior looked a little pale as he climbed up the tree ladder. Now that they'd been in the Shahi village for a couple days, Katjin still clung to walls and railings and rarely ventured near the edge of any of the platforms. Darkest night, the only reason why Katjin actually consented to stay in one of the Shahi huts was because of his fear of rolling out of the tent one night and plummeting to his death on the forest floor below.

To his credit, Katjin tried. He tried really hard, imitating Soren's brave face and trying not to feed the animals below by puking every time he ventured near the edge. Mikael was just happy to be out in fresh air again. The vast flatness of the Horse Clans' plains made him feel like the sky was swallowing him whole. It was just too big, too much space, too great a horizon.

The third obstacle was the Shahi themselves. They were an odd lot, and that was saying something. Mikael had been born in a small 'border' town on the edge of the plains, and then raised in an even smaller family holding about as far away from everything as possible. He was used to isolation and keeping to himself, especially since his father's idea of protection had seemed to be to distance the family from everyone. It surprised him when Tai, Mandric's friend and their first 'real' Shahi contact, actually took them into his home—his hirh, the small huts that Shahi all seemed to live in. Of course, that also meant sharing a living space slightly bigger than a yer with Tai's son, Aidan, who they hadn't met yet, but seemed to be somewhere between Mik's age and Soren's.

Aside from their short time in the Highlandfolk camp, Mikael had spent most of his time either cramped into a small goat-hair tent with Katjin and Soren, or trapped in a dark hole in the ground. The yer hadn't caused too many night terrors after the first few nights, and throughout their summer in the valley, Katjin and Soren had been happy enough to sleep with the tent-flap open, if only to get fresh hair into the small space. While Mikael had grown up living surrounded by solid stone walls and a heavy roof, he wasn't sure how he felt about what looked like a glorifed wattle-and-daub hut, the likes of which hadn't been seen in the Lowlands in years. Especially since said hut—hirh—was perched in the crook of a tree.

There had been protests from both Kat and Soren, since a permanent structure with walls apparently insulted Horse Clan ancestors or some rot. Even if Mik hadn't been a heart-sense, the fear and tension coming off of those two was obvious to even the most 'pathically blind. Tai, however, didn't seem to notice, even when Mandric warned him, over and over, that it might not be such a good idea. Tai's hirh was right at the center of the hirhai—the village itself—and all around him, Mikael could feel the ebb and flow of emotions just waiting to drown him. It was exhausting.

So Tai fed them some kind of gamey-tasting stew that they all kind of picked at, and let them set up their bedrolls in a small room off his hirh. It wasn't so much a good-night as a dismissal. Even ventilated as the room was by the window set high in the wooden wall, it still seemed cramped to Mikael, especially after the loose walls of the yer, that would sometimes billow in the wind. Tired as he was, all he could do was lay awake and try not to thrash around at night. He and Katjin still bound their hands at night, just so that one didn't wake up to the pain that came whenever they physically separated, which meant his days of tossing and turning were over.

One moment, he was staring at the flickers of light the small lamp made on the thatched roof. The next...

Darkness engulfed him. It smothered him, stealing his away. He tried to inhale, but hot, fetid air wrapped around him, holding him down. It sat on his chest like a stone, until each breath was harder and harder to force out. He pushed, pushed, trying to claw it off his face. Opening his mouth to scream—

"Mik!" Cold water hit his face, and Mikael gasped. The crisp night air flooded his lungs and Mikael grasped at the darkness, trying to find the light. Hands pried his eyelids open and he screamed, his throat burning, his voice only a hoarse gasp.

"Mik, Mik," the voice said, over and over. It was a soft refrain now, sounding as pained as his own voice. A light flashed somewhere, coming so close that it was almost blinding. Mikael tried to shield himself with his hands.

"Katjin!"

He opened his eyes, frantically looking around for Kat. Soren stood over his and Katjin's pallet, a waterskin in his hands.

"You were screaming." Soren shivered. He dropped to his knees beside them, rocking back and forth. "You were screaming bad—worse than that time in camp."

Worse than the time he and Katjin had caused an entire Highlandfolk camp to spontaneously fall to the ground, weeping, and Mandric had to knock them out to get it to stop.

Mikael groaned. Next to him, Katjin blinked, bleary-eyed. "Do you think—" He sounded just as rocked and afraid as Mikael felt.

Then they heard the pounding of feet on the wooden pathways, and the door to their room was flung open. Tai, carrying another lamp, stared at them, a boy who had to be Aidan peering over Tai's shoulder.

"What happened?"

Then Mandric's voice, and the sounds of others.

"Mikael? Katjin, are you all right?" Mandric pushed past Tai and Aidan, filling the small room with his looming presence. Mikael automatically shrank back, expecting— not expecting the concern he was faced with.

Mandric knelt, holding out a hand. Katjin struggled with the blankets and with Mikael until he was between Mikael and the rest of the world, even Soren hovering protectively on Mikael's other side.

"Lads, we don't mean any harm," Mandric continued in the same soft voice. "We just want to know that you're all right, that you're not—"

"What *happened*?" Tai repeated, still standing in the doorway. "Mandric, you never said anything about—"

"That's because you didn't listen, you idiot!" Mandric said over his shoulder. "You didn't listen when I told you that having them around others could be a dangerous situation. I told you what happened in the camp. I told you what happened to the cavalry."

Mikael leaned into Katjin's side, burying his face in Katjin's shoulder in shame. He could feel a light kiss on his forehead, and Katjin's arm wrapping protectively around him. "I didn't mean it," Mikael muttered, not knowing what else to say. The fear fled, almost as quickly as it had surrounded him. Now, the air buzzed with puzzlement and questions, more annoyance than fear.

"I think the lads need their own place to stay. Maybe one of the outer hirh," At the sound of Mandric's voice, Mikael peeked over Katjin's shoulder. Mandric's anger was directed more at Tai than them. "Too much exposure like this won't help them, or the hirhai either."

"We can't leave them alone," Tai said, remaining in the doorway. "A bonded pair must be supervised. Otherwise you never know what sort of…incidents might occur."

Both Mandric and Tai seemed to look and not look at Aidan at the same time. Aidan, always in his father's shadow, appeared to be oblivious.

Soren spoke up. "Maybe you should trust us. Unless, y'know, you want this to happen again."

Mandric chuckled. "He's got a point."

They were hustled out of the hirh, blankets and all, and dragged through the darkness. Limited to the light of lanterns and lamps, you almost couldn't tell you were so high up in the trees. Katjin seemed a little more relaxed.

"We don't have an empty hirh, but we can put them on one of the practice platforms for the rest of the night," Tai was telling Mandric. "Empty out a hirh tomorrow."

"If you've got some kind of leather or skins, we could probably make a hirh," Soren said, one arm holding up Mikael and the other hauling a pile of bedding. "We'll be okay, sleeping out tonight."

Mandric nodded. "Should be dawn soon anyway."

Looking back over his shoulder, Mikael could see a line of pale Shahi, almost ghostly in the dim light of their lamps, staring at them as they went. The Shahi's faces were carefully blank, as if they didn't want to show their judgement. Mikael could read it, though: the fear, the uncertainty, the nervousness. Apparently they had some experience with bonded pairs, if what Mandric and Tai said were true, but it must not have been a good experience.

The line of Shahi surrounded the edge of the low platform they were finally led to, watching as if to make sure that Mikael would stay as far away as possible. Mik supposed it could be worse, since the platform at least wasn't a hole in the ground, and wooden floorboards were warmer than the cold ground ever was.

"Can they go away now?" Mikael muttered to Mandric as they settled in their bedrolls. "It's—"

"Creepy," Katjin supplied, curling up against Mikael's back. He yawned. "I don't think I'll sleep a..."

And then Katjin snored.

Mikael rolled his eyes at Soren, who cracked a grin. "If you ignore them, they might go away," Soren pointed out, fluffing up his own small pillow and rearranging the blankets to his liking.

As if they understood Soren's words, the Shahi faded into the trees that shrouded the dark pathways of the hirhai.

"Sleep, lad," Mandric said softly, setting up his own bedroll on the other side of Soren. "We'll deal with it in the morning."

Mikael swallowed. That's what he was afraid of.

There didn't seem to be many repercussions. The Shahi as a group avoided them. Tai and Aidan cleaned out the hirh that Mikael and Soren and Katjin had slept next to, and then, as promised, provided them with what was available for building a yer, if they wanted. Then, Tai and Mandric disappeared somewhere, obviously going to decide Mikael and Katjin's future.

Tai's son, however, was a different matter…

"You've got an admirer," Katjin had muttered as they tried to piece together a tent from the bits of oiled hide the Shahi brought them. Even Soren was complaining about the unwieldiness of the heavy leather.

Mikael looked up from his shoddy stitches to finally get a good look at the haughty Shahi staring at them. The fella was obviously Shahi; he had the short, slight build and the tell-tale red hair. From what Mikael could see of the leather-clad figure, there were no wings or tails or horns or other signs of demon-birth, but the fella's eyes were the same queer yellow-gold as Tai's. Katjin's eyes were hazel-green, always laughing and generally cheerful. This one's eyes—this alien Shahi's eyes—made Mikael believe in every story he'd ever heard of the Shahi demons and the Lowlander babies they seemed to eat and thrive on.

"Aidan," the Shahi said, pounding his chest with his fist before holding both hands out, as if to push the three of them away.

Mikael couldn't help staring, not sure if he should get up and push this Aidan off the platform they sat on or just ignore him. It was strange. He could read at least the surface emotions of most people he met—that was what being a heart sense was all about—but Aidan seemed to be an emotional void. Emotions usually assaulted him until his ears almost bled, but from Aidan, it was almost a pleasant relief. That wasn't Katjin's usual shielding trick either. Mik got nothing off of Aidan, and that kind of frightened him. He'd felt the emotions of others around him every moment of every day for the past few years, possibly longer, and the fact that he could read this one strange fella worried him.

Before he could make a decision, though, Soren decided to act for them. As oldest of the trio, Soren had declared it his responsibility to keep Mik and Katjin safe. What had started out as a familial obligation set on him by Kat and Soren's grandparents had apparently turned into some kind of personal mission. While waves of mild annoyance still rolled off of Soren on occasion, Katjin's older cousin seemed to look at the two of them with genuine fondness now. That still boggled Mikael's mind, but he wasn't about to look a gift Horse Clansman in the mouth.

Soren stood, stretching to his full height of over two strides. To Mikael's satisfaction, Soren towered over Aidan by almost a full head. Granted, that made Aidan about his and Katjin's height, but still.

Walking toward the Shahi, Soren touched his own chest and said, "Soren." Then Soren placed his hands, palms forward, against Aidan's. Aidan's fingers curled over Soren's, linking their hands together, palm to palm. The Shahi looked a little relieved, losing a bit of his haughtiness. Not all of it, though. Aidan nodded his head toward Mikael and Katjin, and Mikael couldn't help feeling like he was being dismissed.

Soren was probably trying to find an excuse to pry their fingers apart. Mikael could almost see those fingers flexing in protest to Aidan's tight grip. Anxiety washed over Soren and his mouth grew tight. Beside Mikael, Katjin started to chuckle, Kat's own anxiety lightening some.

"Katjin," Mikael's bonded said, pointing first at himself, then Mikael. "Mikael." Mikael proprietarily linked his fingers through Kat's, giving Aidan a pointed look.

Aidan's eyebrows arched, some expression of surprise and acceptance crossing his face, and he nodded. "Soren. Katjin. Mikael," he repeated dutifully. Then, slowly, "Horse Clan."

Mikael was still working on his proficiency with Clantongue. Soren spoke passing Lowlander, and Katjin was fluent, but most of their conversations over the past months had been in Clantongue for everyone's comfort. Being an empath didn't seem to help too much with the language barrier; you probably had to be a thought-sense for that to be of any use. Now, adding a third language to the mix was probably going to make things interesting. Especially since it seemed like only Tai spoke any Clantongue of consequence, let alone Lowlander.

Soren and Katjin looked at Mikael, as if they expected him to make a decision. Was he still a Lowlander? He'd been adopted into the Horse Clans by blood-rite and more or less physically bound to Katjin in the process. His own Lowlander family had squirreled him away like a leper once they figured out that his 'pathy was manifesting. And the Empire that guarded and arguably protected Lowlanders, Horse Clan and Highlandfolk had kidnapped and tried to kill him. While the Horse Clans hadn't exactly welcomed him in with open arms, they had at least tried to protect him.

So he nodded. "Horse Clan." The black dye had

finally faded from his blond hair, but Aidan probably hadn't met very many 'real' Clanfolk, so Mikael wasn't going to worry. Though there were obvious differences between Soren and Katjin's bronzed, wide-cheeked faces and almond-shaped eyes and his own paleness and non-Clan features, Mikael wasn't going to push the issue.

Aidan finally let go of Soren's hands, much to Soren's obvious relief. He moved closer, kicking at the pile of awkwardly stitched hides. "Hirh," he said, nodding toward one of the small, thatched huts that perched so precariously in the crotches of the surrounding trees. "Hirhai," and then he said something in Shahi. Hands fluttered at his face, mimicking crying. "Hirhai," he repeated, and then screamed bloody murder.

Mikael felt his face heat up. "Thanks for telling us," he muttered, looking at the ground. One more reason to stay in a tent as far from the hirhai itself as possible. That pretty much confirmed the fact that the feeling was mutual; the Shahi wanted them to stay as far away as well.

But that apparently wasn't Aidan's only point. He walked over to the hirh and knocked on the door, pretending to go inside. "Hirh," he said again, as if insisting on something.

Whatever it was, Katjin caught on. "Not sleeping in there, thank you," he said, shaking his head. Mikael could almost hear the litany that was probably going through Katjin's head: no walls, no roof, no trees, no way.

Kat had mentioned, numerous times, that even when he and his traveling-merchant/sometimes spy father went down into the Lowlands to trade, they always stayed in their yer, their tent. Katjin's fear of solid walls extended to anything that might block their ability to escape: trees, fences, large rocks, caves. Mikael was surprised they'd survived as long as they did in that narrow valley of theirs. They'd spent nearly four moons there, by his own count. Maybe the novelty of their emotional and physical bond, and the fact that they couldn't exist without physically touching in some way, had occupied Katjin's attention and taken his mind off of it.

Aidan looked amused for some reason. "Hirh," he repeated with a smirk before turning away and striding off toward the main village. From the angle of their own lonely hut off to the side, Mikael could see that the hirhai was set up in rough concentric rings around a main platform area. Wood and rope bridges and ladders of all kinds linked the different rings and platforms. They had been given a platform further back from the main platform, allowing them an unobstructed view of the whole village, what there was of it. The hirhai seemed about the size of his own home village..

When they were still sitting around the pile of hide, trying to make sense of some kind of tent a sun's span later—though it was hard to judge how much of a hand's span the sun had moved in the sky, since he couldn't exactly see the sun for all the trees—Mandric also came by. "I hear you met Aidan," the Highlandfolk said with a grin. It didn't take a 'path to tell that he was amused.

Mikael shrugged. "I guess." He glared at the hide, which didn't seem to give way to any of the needles he tried. "Can't we just stay in the hirh?" He knew he was whining, but at this point, his back hurt, his hands were cramped, and all he really wanted to do was sit in a real chair and sleep in a real bed. Even if it did mean a repeat of last night. Sleeping on the wooden platform outside under the trees hadn't been as comforting as he thought it would be, especially with Katjin and Soren twitching at every noise that came out of the forest.

He watched Katjin survey their hapless laps of hide. Katjin's hand found Mikael's thigh under the pile of leather, squeezing lightly. At least anxiety took Katjin's mind off of the events of the past seven days. Any emotion was better than the black sorrow that Katjin had carried through their entire trip over the mountains into the Shahi forests.

"Walls carry ghosts," his bonded said softly, so quietly that Mikael almost didn't hear it. "Apa always said that Lowlanders are haunted by ghosts because their walls keep the spirits of the ancestors in."

Mikael tried not to think of the stone cellar, of the dark and the way the feelings had echoed off those solid walls, penning him in with only his shouts and cries and bloody fists for company. Stone was solid, never weathered, wouldn't burn in the fires of raging Horse Clans come down from their plains. The Lowlanders learned that lesson well enough after seasons of Clan raids, to the point that the Empire had actually forbid wooden buildings outside of the walled cities.

"Wood walls don't last forever," Mikael said, his hand finding Katjin's and squeezing it tight. He tried to project the same calming feelings that Kat used so often on him. "Wood falls to dust. It's mortal, like we are."

Both Soren and Katjin seemed to consider this.

"You can chop your way through it," Soren offered, sharing his cousin's fear of being hemmed in by anything but a woven tent.

"It won't leak," Mikael added, kicking at the heavy waterproof leather. From the sheer mass of moss that hung from everything, and the dampness in the air, he got the impression that it rained a lot here. It was hotter, too, this side of the mountain, for all it was approaching autumn back on the plains and in Stoneridge.

Finally, Katjin nodded. "You don't have the right stuff to make a proper yer here anyway."

Mikael couldn't help sighing in relief. He thought it was a little silly of him, the sheer thrill that had flushed through him at the sight of the little hut, with its door and its windows and its promise of a proper bed and maybe a proper chair and table. He couldn't remember the last time he actually sat at a table, and he wasn't sure what made him feel worse: the simple delight at the prospect of it, or the fact that he didn't even really know how much time had passed.

"Been a long time, aye?" Katjin asked in a low voice. Katjin didn't know everything—starless hells, Mikael wasn't sure *he* knew everything—but Kat definitely *knew*. Understood. Which made Mikael that much more fond of him. Maybe even loved him, on some level. That was one more reason to want to actually stay in the hirh. Huts probably had more than one room, and more than one room meant not sharing a sleeping space with Kat's sometimes-jealous and always-watching cousin.

Mik just smiled a little and shrugged. "Aye, probably." It had all gone so hazy so fast, the sheer weight of the emotions overcrowding his mind until he hadn't really known anything but fever and confusion and the constant onslaught of how other people felt. He wasn't even really sure who had carried him down into the cellar on that day. It might have been Father. It could have been the seneschal, Stephan, who had been nominally in charge of keeping track of Mikael and his tutors, once he was too old for a nurse. There was so much that he didn't remember—one moment, in his bed and the next, clawing for light in that dank cellar, wondering where everyone had gone and why they'd abandoned him.

He could only hope that his family wasn't in the same place as Kat's family, his meke and febe and aunties and uncles and cousins who had all been stolen away or worse by the Empire. There was still a chance that Mother and Father and Mikael's sisters had run, just as he had.

"I'll tell you about it someday," Mik said finally, noticing the shadows under Katjin's greeny-gold eyes. They all had their burdens to bear. They all had their vendettas against the Empire. But while Katjin wanted to go back and right it all, Mikael wasn't so sure. That wasn't a decision that they could make yet, though, not when they'd just figured out where to sleep.

Mikael knew he was somewhere around sixteen years old. He knew he had been born in the 487th year of the Empire, and that it would be simple enough to ask either Kat or Soren the year to find out exactly how much time had passed. He knew they'd been on the plains for nearly five moons, and that equinox had either passed or would pass soon. The exact year, though… Somehow, he didn't want to, though, just because that would make it all the more real.

He wasn't nobility, but his father's family had been landed merchants for generations. Father traveled a little, but not nearly as much as Katjin's Apa. Mother's family came from the Plains, not that anyone ever discussed that. Two of Mik's sisters actually had the sharp cheekbones and slightly-tilted eyes that came from their Horse Clan great-grandmother, but there was no local society to speak of who would actually gossip and wonder about it.

His oldest sister would sometimes talk about the old house, when their family had actually lived in town. Stoneridge hadn't been much to speak of, as far as trade, but it was the only substantial town anywhere near that end of the Plains and the stony bits of the Highlands that encircled it. According to his sisters, Father had moved the family just before Mikael's birth. No one had lived at the country house, a full two-days' ride from Stoneridge, in two generations. Most of Father's relatives preferred what society Stoneridge offered, if anyone could call it that. In Emera's opinion, their family's social status had ended the day Mikael was born, because they'd moved out of that circle of influence. Mikael's three older sisters, all more than five years older than he was, were left to a life of 'loneliness and degradation', as Emera was so fond of dramatizing.

It hadn't been a lonely life. Mikael remembered tutors and fencing instructors and rides on his pony. There had been the occasional trip to Stoneridge for festivals, when Mikael had worn a bandage on his hand to not arouse any suspicions about the fact that he was unbranded. Any unbranded citizen of the Empire was automatically taken into custody to be tested for any 'pathic talents. Why an Empire 'path hadn't branded him at birth just as they did every other baby born within the borders was something Mikael had wondered for years. It was almost as if his parents suspected that he'd develop 'pathy late.

It could've been worse, though. Apparently Katjin's ama had also been a latent 'path. Most 'paths were born with their abilities already in full evidence, taken from their families at birth so that the Empire could raise—

and train—them up properly, so that they could better serve their Empire. Katjin's Lowlander grandmother and grandfather lost other children to the Empire, so they'd decided to nip any potential problems in the bud by taking Kat's ama to the Shahi to have them burn her 'pathy out. Which was how Katjin's Apa met his Ama, smuggling 'paths out of the Empire over to the Shahi for safety.

Which might explain Katjin's absolute terror at anything that related to the Shahi, including their huts.

"We don't have to," he said as he and Katjin sat outside the hirh, leaning up against the rough-hewn wall. He'd seen the occasional wooden shed in Stoneridge, but the hirh walls seemed to be made of deadfall and other broken branches, woven together and stuck with mud instead of the wooden planks the Lowlanders occasionally used. Lowlanders built. Shahi buildings just seemed to grow from the trees themselves.

Katjin looked at him, those green eyes studying him. "We do," Kat said finally. "Soren and me have to stop being stubborn about things. Trying to put up an ancestors-damned tent won't get us any closer to finding out what happened to Meke and Febe." He bit his lip. Again, that overwhelming wave of guilt and grief almost overwhelmed Mikael.

"Stop it," Mikael said flatly, shaking Katjin. "It's not your fault. If it's anyone's fault, it's mine." If it was anyone's fault at all, it was his family's, for not having him branded at birth in the first place. Would life as an Empire 'path really have been that bad, if he hadn't know the difference?

Katjin started to shake his head, but Mikael caught Kat's chin in one hand, bringing Katjin's face in close. He leaned his forehead against Kat's, looking his bonded directly in the eye. "You didn't know. Your Meke and Febe didn't know. It's not…" He swallowed, trying not to think of the grandparents he'd never met and would probably never remember. "We're family now, and we're going to stick together and—"

Chapped lips covered his, kissing him hungrily. As if Mikael couldn't read that emotion easily enough, especially from his own stiffness. That was something else he'd have to deal with eventually—his other attachments to Katjin. It was one thing to try to avoid touch, as he had these past four moons. Now, he hungered for Katjin's touch and wanted to drown in it until there was nothing left of him.

Not if it meant drowning in sorrow, though. He had enough sorrow of his own.

"You're trying to distract me," Katjin complained in a breathless voice, once they broke the kiss. "You're—"

"Disgusting me," Soren said, popping his head out from the doorway of the hirh. "Just come in, you dumb babies. Walls aren't as bad as you'd think."

Not that Soren had closed the door or the windows of the hirh while he'd been inside.

Mik shot a look at Katjin, warming inside at the grin he got in return. "Ready?" he asked, pulling Katjin to his feet.

Katjin took a deep breath and then nodded. "Ready."

There wasn't much to the hirh. It was one room below, with a sleeping loft above. They had a table and a couple of benches, some shelves hung against the wall and a fireplace to cook at. A ladder leaned up against the wall to the right of the door, obviously leading to the loft above. Two open windows let in plenty of light and air. From the look of things, there was even a window up in the loft—no glass, which meant Katjin would always be able to feel the breeze on his face. There would be time later to wonder about what Shahi did when it rained, unless they had some kind of oiled paper that they used to block the rain.

Soren had already unrolled his blankets, choosing a spot in front of the fireplace. "You two can have the loft," he said, waving a hand at the ladder.

"You even been up there?" Katjin eyed the ladder as if it was damned by the ancestors themselves. "You haven't."

Mikael couldn't help laughing at the dark red color that spread across Soren's tanned cheeks. "Maybe not," Soren muttered, looking at the floor. "Why don't you go up?"

A determined look on his face, Katjin faced the ladder. He looked back at Mikael, who shrugged. "If you climb up fast, and I go after you, we should be okay." That was something he'd never considered, climbing a ladder with one hand, or trying to follow the person in front of you while still keeping a hold of them somehow. If the Shahi could fix that somehow...

He knew what they were going to work on next, at least. It would be nice to have a hand to himself again. They'd gotten to the point where their blood bond seemed to be satisfied if the two of them were just sitting next to each other. The next step, though, was actual personal space, not that Mikael could actually remember personal space.

Which was a good thing, since the loft, when he got up there, was barely more than a square of plank floor four strides by four strides, set under the sloping roof. There was a short wall closing off the fourth wall, so at least they wouldn't roll off the loft and down onto Soren on the floor one night. No bed, but a floor was still more than Mikael had hoped for. And with the pile of rugs and furs that were rolled up under the small window, it would probably be comfortable enough—as comfortable as his pallet in the yer had been, to say the least.

He looked at Katjin, who looked back at him. They could only stand up straight in the middle, just under the peak of the roofline. That meant they were the perfect distance for just kind of gazing into each other's eyes, because that was what you did with your bonded... partner... lover? Person. Someday, he'd figure out the title. Someday, he'd figure out a lot of things.

"Cozy, eh?" Katjin asked, blushing a little. He was cute when he blushed. "And alone. Yup, we're definitely alone."

"I can still hear you!" Soren called up from below. "So don't get too excited." There was a long pause as the blush deepened more and more on Katjin's tanned face. "Or if you are, don't tell me about it."

"Nobody said you were invited anyway," Mikael yelled back with a grin. Suddenly, he felt good. He felt right. He felt...

Free.

Just because, he swept Katjin up in a big hug, holding Katjin's slightly shorter body close. He hugged and held and tried to imbue everything of the past four months. He hoped he wasn't overwhelming Katjin; the emotions were one-thing firsthand. Secondhand, he could only guess how intense it would be.

Kat's arms came around him, and then a mouth shyly touched his neck and under his ear. It tickled. He couldn't help laughing a little bit, enough that Katjin actually pulled back.

"What?" Kat asked, eyes confused.

"Tickles," Mikael said, squirming away a little. "No one's tickled me in…"

Silence—not just the sound of silence, but the feeling of utter emotional deprivation. "We're fixing that," Katjin said in that soft, fierce voice of his. "It's on the list." Right after 'find out what happened to our families' and right before 'take down the Empire.' If anyone else had asked, Mikael didn't know what he would've said, but it was Katjin, and Kat meant everything to him. He'd do anything for Katjin, even sleep on the floor of a treehouse in a village inhabited by the demons that had haunted his childhood.

"Now, we should fix this, though," Mikael said, the emotions getting to be a little too much. He could only take so much of the grief/guilt/worry that seemed to exude from Katjin so often now. Kissing, though, that always seemed to make those feelings go away.

Sure, it caused other feelings too, but neither of them were protesting too much.

Kat's mouth was warm and clumsy, but Mik didn't mind, not even when their heads knocked a bit because they'd both leaned the same way at the same time. This was Katjin, and this was touch, and this was maybe even love, if he thought—or didn't think—about it too much. This was life and light and feeling. Starless hells, but there were a lot of feelings now, a lot of emotion. He didn't mind the overwhelmingness then, just because it meant he was alive.

One hand cupped the back of Katjin's head, tangling in Kat's straight dark hair. The other held Kat by the shoulder, pulling him closer and closer until they almost merged into one. He could feel one of Katjin's hands drifting down his back, almost to his arse. Katjin squeezed, which make Mikael squeak in surprise.

"I don't wanna know!" was Soren's loud comment.

Mikael grinned at Katjin, who smiled that sunny smile back. Soren was right. There were some some things Katjin's cousin just didn't need to know.

That night was strange. Shahi food wasn't quite what he'd expected: some kind of ground fowl, some kind of root vegetable and bread made from nut flour. It was surprisingly good, and he was just happy to have bird again. He couldn't remember the last time he'd had something that wasn't cow or goat or wild game. Even if the ground fowl wasn't chicken, it still tasted really good, especially stuffed with garlic and onions as it had been. The wooden plate seemed light to his hands, usually used to stoneware at home, and the utensils were clumsy, but at least he wasn't eating with his hands and knife as they had in the Clan and Highlandfolk camp.

Tai had brought them dinner. Mikael thought he caught sight of Aidan just outside the door, but couldn't be sure. As soon as Tai set the food down, though, it started to rain. He'd shown them how to latch the shutters closed to keep the rain from getting in. With the lanterns lit and a fire going in the fireplace to ward off the chill of the rain, the hirh was cozy. They kept the door open a crack, though, just because Soren and Katjin kept eyeing the walls as if they expected them to close in at any moment.

Not knowing what to do with the empty plates, they left them on the wooden platter just inside the door.

"They could just sit out in the rain," Soren pointed

out. "Easier to wash them, that way."

"But what if they aren't treated wood? They could get all rotten, and then the Shahi might curse us or something." Katjin shuttered. "Can't we open the door again? I don't mind if I get wet."

Soren unrolled his bedroll without a fuss, not so much a worry emanating from him for once. Mikael wasn't sure why Soren was so calm, but he wasn't questioning it. The rain stopped just as they were getting ready to go to bed, so the windows and door were opened once again. That seemed to have a calming effect on Katjin as well, as if the knowledge that he could leave at any time almost made up for the fact that he was closed in.

By mutual consent, they slept with one of the lanterns going, sitting on top of the table down below. Even with the low wall separating off the loft, Mikael could still just make out the circle of its light on the underside of the thatch roof. That meant he could still see Kat's face if he needed to. They'd never had anything but darkness inside the yer, but somehow, it hadn't mattered in there. Maybe it was the seeming fragility of the yer itself, since it was little more than woven-horsehair sides wrapped around a wooden lattice. The hirh was definitely sturdier, but the yer had been a little more comforting, if only because it could easily be moved if they needed to hide somewhere else. As if anyone would find them here, deep in the Shahi forests. As if anyone was trying to find them.

"Do you think they're still looking?" he asked Katjin as they laid out their bedrolls, arranging the pile of blankets and furs next to each other.

Katjin shrugged as he punched his pillow into shape. "Don't know. Apa said he'd get word to us if he found out anything—I guess Mandric makes the trip regular between the Highlands and here."

Mikael snorted. "So much for no one being in contact with the Shahi in generations." That was another Empire myth burnt to the ground.

Katjin lay down on the pallet and Mikael followed. Someone had thoughtfully placed a necessary pot in the corner, which meant they wouldn't have to go down the ladder in the dark or attempt to piss out the window. He could only imagine what might happen if he tried to find a privy in the middle of the night, and apparently leaking over the railing on any of the platforms was frowned upon. There was no privy, as such, in their hirh, but Tai had said something about a communal privy somewhere, and using the trunk of the tree to filter out the wasteful parts as it worked its way down to the root system. Then it got a little too technical and detailed from there, something Mikael really didn't need to know about. In any case, he was glad they were covered if need be in the middle of the night.

"It makes me wish I'd paid more attention," Katjin said, studying his fingers. Kat was always fidgeting with something; Soren said it was Kat's overabundance of energy, getting the better of him. "Finding out from Mandric and Tai that apparently Apa's involved in a great anti-Empire conspiracy, and that it's been going on for years and years…"

Mikael wrapped his hands around Katjin's, interlacing their fingers. His hands looked so pale next to Katjin's, even after a summer of sunshine. And his fingers were still so bony too. "We weren't supposed to know. What was your apa going to do, confide in you? He didn't even confide in Soren, and Soren's grown."

There was a flash of a smile, and a bit of content

seemed to ease the tension that tied both Kat and Mik's stomachs up in knots. "Apa didn't even want to take me to the Highlands this summer," Katjin said with a slight smile, squeezing Mikael's fingers. Then he sighed, the smile faltering. Again, there was that internal war between content and unease that Katjin constantly seemed to be battling.

"We'll find them," Mikael said, pulling Katjin close. "We'll find them."

Without any other words to say, they lay back on the pallets, fingers still intertwined. Mikael rolled over, nosing Katjin's ear. "Will you be able to sleep? We can drag our blankets outside."

Hands touched his face lightly. "I think I'll be all right."

And then something howled an unholy racket, sounding as if it were right under their hirh. Mikael had to remember for a moment that they were a hundred lengths or more up in the air.

"Kat? I hope that was you..." Soren called out from below. "Um, mind if I close the door?"

"I think I'll stay inside tonight," Katjin muttered, curling up closer to Mikael. "Maybe that's why Shahi live in trees..."

"Mik." Someone elbowed him. "Mik, wake *up*."

Mikael flung his arm out, trying to push whoever it was away. Couldn't be one of his sisters, since they were too old for that kind of nonsense. Not even Emera—

He swallowed, suddenly wide awake. Emera was his next oldest sister, still nearly five years older than he was. Out of his three sisters, she'd always been the most sympathetic to him and the least resentful. Their older sisters, Mei and Lina, rarely did anything but complain about the society that they were missing—the parties, the dances, the possible matches—living so far out in the country. Emera, though, had always tried to take time to spend some time with him, even if she didn't understand all the fuss and the secrecy. Mei was the only other one that Mother had taught the aiding song to.

"Mikael, come on." It was Katjin's voice, soft and high in the darkness. Every day, it cracked and crowed its way up and down the key, but never settled. Katjin would never be a singer—which was probably better for the entire Empire. That was a problem, though, since Katjin was constantly humming tunelessly under his breath.

"What's going on?" Mikael asked, rubbing at his eyes. From the dim light of the lantern below, he could barely see. It was obviously still dark, which made him wonder what Katjin was doing at this hour. "Just piss in the pot. We'll empty it tomorrow."

"It's not that," Katjin insisted. "Just… listen." As hard as Mikael tried, he couldn't feel any fear coming off of Katjin, nor hysteria of any kind. Mikael's blood seemed to course faster, as if the staccato beat of Katjin's heart was causing his own to speed up. But that was more excitement than anything else.

He was about to tell Katjin to shove it, turn over and go to sleep, when he heard it. There was that cackle again, sounding like something was laughing hysterically right below their hirh. The cackled continued until a howl that gave Mikael goosebumps, followed by a huge WHOMP!

"Wha?" Soren's sleepy voice called up. "Kat? You snoring again?"

"Didn't Mandric say something about birds and cats—giant ones?" Katjin asked, almost vibrating with excitement now.

"Moah," Mikael said, trying to remember. "And nari? Something like that."

"I think one of the cats just got a bird." Katjin's eyes were wide in the lantern light, almost feverish. "You never hear anything like that on the plains." From the fear in Katjin's eyes earlier, Mikael thought that Katjin would never venture outside the hirh at night. Now, he wasn't so sure. Then again, common sense didn't always seem to be one of Kat's strong points.

"Okay, so you heard your monster bird. It's still dark, so go back to sleep!" This time, the thud against the floor of the loft came from Soren tossing something at them. "Good night."

As Katjin settled back against Mikael, Mikael stared up at the shadows flickering in and out of the weave of the thatch above their heads. He didn't think that he would've missed the wind rustling in the trees, or the sounds leaves made against a wall or a window at night. The country house had been surrounded by trees, their own small woods creating a park for playing in and having adventures when he was a child. Being back here, among the trees again, almost made him feel like he was at home—as long as he ignored the weird howling and the man-eating cats that apparently prowled the forest floor.

Chapter Two

They were up early on the second day. With no camp to break and no horses to tend to, Katjin and Soren looked a little bit lost. Katjin kept looking over his shoulder, as if he was expecting his horse Shanti to appear out of nowhere. There was one more brick of guilt to add to the wall; Katjin had to leave his beloved horse behind, the one who had carried him for years now, when they went over the mountain to the Shahi forests. Though it had only been half a moon-span now, Mik thought, since they left the Highland camp on the other side, it still seemed like a lifetime.

This time, it was Aidan that came by with their breakfast. Instead of the yogurt and other Clanfolk white food that he'd become accustomed to eating in the morning, breakfast here was some kind of porridge dowsed with honey and studded with dried berries. Mikael's stomach rumbled at the mere scent of it. To sit at a real table and eat porridge out of a bowl and with a spoon... He hadn't realized what a city boy he was until he'd found himself in a Clan camp with only Soren and Kat and three horses for company.

Aidan grinned at the sound of Mikael's stomach

rumbling, looking a lot friendlier this morning than he had yesterday. "Hungry," was his only comment as he set down the bowls. "You, Mikael. You eat." Then, with an almost indifferent nod, he said, "Soren and Katjin eat."

Mikael grabbed a bowl, sitting down on the bench. "Porridge?" He pointed to the dried fruit. "Berries?"

The Shahi stared at him for a moment, considering. Again, there was that curious blank feeling when Mikael tried to probe Aidan. He couldn't read anything. Even Katjin seemed to notice it, standing behind Mikael as he was. Looking over his shoulder, Mikael could see a look of concentration on Katjin's face, as if Kat himself was trying to read something off of Aidan—anything, really.

"Porridge," Aidan said slowly. "Breakfast is porridge. With berries." Again, Mikael couldn't help but wonder if Aidan was reading something off him, the same way the 'paths had back in the cavalry camp.

"'Path?" Katjin asked suddenly, touching his head. "Thought?" Then he touched his chest. "Heart?"

Those strange yellow eyes now turned to stare at Katjin, who puffed up his chest and glowered at the Shahi boy. Aidan stretched out one arm and lightly touched Mikael over the heart. "Heart 'path?" he asked, ignoring Katjin.

Mikael nodded. "Heart-sense." Then he reached behind him and took Katjin's hand. "Bound to Kat." He held up his free hand for Aidan to see, the scars on his wrist white against what he had of a tan.

This time, Aidan's arm swung toward Katjin, touching Katjin lightly. "Katjin is heart 'path with?"

Exchanging a look with Katjin, Mikael nodded. "We're 'paths together, tied together."

That seemed to strike some kind of a chord with Aidan, because he nodded suddenly, as if everything was clear. He rattled off something in Shahi and said something about black and gold, which made no sense. Then he smiled, and the smile made all the difference in his almost alien face.

"Bound." Aidan showed off his palm proudly, and Mikael could see a scar similar to his own crossing the calloused palm. Katjin breathed a sigh of relief, which Mikael didn't even know how to interpret. Either Aidan had a partner of his own somewhere, or the Shahi tried to use the same kind of blood-binding ritual to bring about some kind of 'pathic bond too.

Aidan's bright grin faded, though. "Were. Was. Was?" Mikael nodded at the correct form of the verb. "Was bound. Da—" He made a chopping motion with his hands, as if severing the bond.

Katjin shuddered, and that small feeling of unease sitting at the bottom of Mikael's stomach slowly began its rise to his throat.

There was a shout from outside the door, a voice that Mikael recognized as Tai's. Aidan rolled his eyes, then headed out the door without another word. Mikael looked up and stared at Katjin, not sure what to make of all that.

Soren sank down at the table next to Mikael, grabbing one of the remaining bowls of porridge and shoveling it into his mouth. "Fella's an odd one," he said around a mouthful of breakfast. "Makes you two ducks look almost common." He said it with a grin, which meant it was Soren being funny. At least, though, that made the mood pass.

Katjin stuck his tongue out at Soren, obviously still suffering from the same familial immaturity that they seemed to like to treat each other with. Maybe it was because Mikael never had brothers, or even sisters who really interacted with him more than they had to.

"He's kind of…" Katjin flapped his hand as he sat down between Mikael and Soren, shoving his cousin over.

"Strange?" Mikael suggested, craning his neck to try and peer out the open door. "At least he's talking to us."

"To you," Katjin retorted, starting on his own bowl. "Hey, this is good."

Mikael grinned. "Better'n white food?"

Katjin emphatically shook his head. "Nothing's better than white food. Except maybe Meke's—" Then Katjin clammed up, his eyes dropping to the table. Knots tied up in Mikael's stomach and his eyes began to burn. He never met the woman, but the hazy feelings that Katjin let slip every once in a while seemed filled with nothing but love for her. He'd always thought that his own mother had tried as best she could, even going so far to teach him the Horse Clan aiding song that Mother's grandmother had passed down the family line, in case someone should need it. He'd never felt anything about his mother though that Katjin obviously felt for his meke and febe.

"We'll find 'em, Kat," Soren promised. "And then Meke will make frybread, and the world will be all happy again."

Though he managed a weak smile, not even Katjin looked convinced by that.

Tai sent Aidan for them later. They didn't get much more than a beckoning hand and a command, "Follow with." As if they'd had much choice in the matter. So the three of them followed like ducklings in a row, making their way across the moss-hung tree trunk paths until it seemed like they'd circled around the entire hirhai. Tai and Mandric sat on wooden stools outside a larger hirh, heads bent in serious conversation.

"—sure nothing else from Nolan?" Tai said softly as they came into range. Mikael could feel urgency and impatience radiating of him. "We can't wait—"

"...signs of cavalry revolting as word gets out," Mandric replied in the same quiet tone. "The families were—" He chose that moment to look up, and his mouth shut at the sight of them.

So much for getting more information. Still, Mikael was never so happy in his life to see someone. He had to restrain himself from throwing his arms around Mandric as they approached where the two men sat. "I thought you would've left already," he couldn't help saying as soon as he saw the Highlandfolk.

"Wouldn't leave without saying goodbye. I thought you trusted me more than that, now, lad," Mandric said with a grin. "Besides, you'll see me often enough. I still come to visit my family here."

"We'll be here for a while then?" Soren asked, his voice carefully neutral, though Mikael could feel the tension that ran tight and twisted through it.

"Y'know that, lad," Mandric answered quietly, putting one hand on Soren's shoulder. "I'll talk with your uncle Nolan and we'll see what we can find about Redwind camp, but until then…"

Soren nodded, muttering something about smoke in his eyes and turning away. Before Katjin could say anything, Mikael had an arm around him, humming softly under his breath. That had become a comfort to both of them, even if Katjin's offkey humming seemed more like buzzing to Mikael's ears. He'd grown up singing, since it and swordplay seemed to be the only two things he excelled in as a child.

"Until then," Mandric continued in a gruff voice, "we've got to do something about you lads. And there are some rules you must learn if you're to stay here."

Mikael wanted to roll his eyes. So even the Shahi demons were trying to get rid of him? Katjin smirked slightly, as if he knew exactly what Mikael was thinking—feeling, same difference, these days.

"You know we're having you stay a bit further out than the other hirhai, eh?" Tai asked, leading them outside to the platform that took up most of the crotch of their tree. In the distance, between the branches, Mikael could see the other hirhai clustered in groups around the village center.

"So we won't disturb anyone, or any one us, right?" Katjin asked. He was scowling. "We're not dangerous."

Mandric and Tai exchanged a long glance. Mikael could feel the hesitation, taste the bile-like fear that both men seemed to have in the back of their throats, especially coming from Tai. "That's not what I'd call what happened to the cavalry," Mandric responded slowly, carefully. "And I witnessed that first-hand."

"Mik just threw his emotions is all," Soren said with a shrug. "Then we went and cleaned up the rest. What's wrong with that?"

Tai seemed a little startled by Soren's nonchalance at the whole thing. In fact, those weird yellow eyes of his bugged out a bit. "That's all," he echoed in a sour voice. "Mandric—"

Mandric held up a hand, as if to quiet Tai, and then

motioned for Soren to continue. Instead, though, it was Katjin who took up the thread.

Katjin started tapping his fingers on the platform railing, so agitated that Mik's limbs tensed with the excess energy. "But at the camp. When we…" Katjin trailed off, obviously knowing exactly what the older men were talking about.

"When we broke down," Mikael finished flatly. He looked at Mandric, meeting the Highlandfolk's eyes squarely. "Did any of them die, the cavalry?"

One slow nod was Mandric's only response. "That's the risk, working with 'paths. That's the Empire's bane, breeding and enhancing the gifts as they have." Mandric heaved a long, heavy sigh. "We didn't want to put that on you lads, especially with what's been done to you. But if we don't control this now, before it gets out of hand again, who knows what will happen, especially if the Empire ever manages to get a hold of Mikael and realizes what was done, and what potential he has."

The tapping grew more frantic, Katjin's fingers beating a pace that almost made Mikael cringe. He wanted to grab at those fingers and hold them tight, just to keep them from exploding off Katjin's hands. Tai seemed to be bothered by the tapping as well. The pulse at his throat almost seemed to beat in time with the temp—rat-tat-rat-tat-tat-rat-tat.

"Stop!" Tai smacked Katjin's fingers away as if they burned. "You can't— You can't just *do* that."

It was all Mikael could do to stare at Tai in surprise. Anger built up inside him, welling up to the surface. These men had stolen him from his camp, taken his life as if it was nothing and dragged him across a mountain so he could be 'fixed.' And if he didn't want to be fixed? If he saw nothing wrong with himself and with Kat?

"Easy," Katjin soothed, his fingers stroking the back of Mikael's neck. "Easy." That rumbly humming soothed Mikael, helping his muscles relax. He focused on the soft buzz, letting it calm him.

Tai twitched again, as if the mere presence of the song offended his pointed ears. "That's why," he said, breathing heavily. "That's why we want you to control yourselves. Why we're going to teach you control, just like we teach our own youngsters."

Soren's eyes narrowed. "I thought you didn't have 'paths the way the Empire does." It seemed a little late for scepticism on this, since Soren was the one who involved the Highlandfolk, and then the Shahi in this in the first place.

"We don't have 'paths," Tai said. "At least, we didn't until the 'paths of the Empire crossed our mountains. Our gifts are different. It's, for lack of a better word, magic."

Ah, there was where the baby-eating came in. Mikael eyed the branches, trying to judge the distance to the ground. If he dragged Katjin and ran fast enough…

"Not that kind of magic," Tai said sharply, as if he could read Mik's thoughts. "We don't eat babies under the light of the moon, we don't sacrifice up our grandmothers to the dark gods. It's magic."

To prove his point, he cupped his hand. Chanting something under his breath and tapping out an off-beat rhythm with his foot that almost counterpointed the chant, he concentrated on his hand until it glowed. A small ball of light about the size of an apple coalesced into Tai's hand, growing redder and redder until it was as shiny and glossy as… an apple. Beads of sweat pooled on Tai's forehead, dripping down his pale skin as he closed his eyes. The chanting and rhythm grew frantic, Tai's breath coming harder and harder until—

There was an apple sitting in the palm of his hand.

If the Empire could make things materialize out of thin air, like food or troops or anything, they probably would have materialized themselves over the mountains centuries ago and taken these forests as easily as they took the Lowlands.

"We manipulate the earth's energies and tell it what to do," Tai said, once he'd recovered his breath. "We sing to it, and by singing to it, convince it that it wants to flow in a certain way that it might not have flown before."

"And everyone knows these songs?" Soren asked, eyes wide. "Anyone can do them?"

Mandric shook his head, chuckling. "We call them song-lines. Each family has its own line to sing and its own set of spells it knows to use. If we separate out the knowledge like that, it assures that no one can take advantage of it and use it for ill."

"Like the Empire," Mikael said flatly.

Tai nodded. "Like the Empire."

Katjin leaned forward, and Mikael could almost read the intent in his eyes. "What were your dealings with the Empire, if they're the reason you divided up your spells?"

Tai leaned back against the railing. "I suppose it wouldn't hurt to tell you, since it isn't as if the Empire would have." He glanced at Mandric, who nodded. "Your apa, Katjin, has he told you anything about it?"

Kat snorted. "Apa didn't even think I should know that Ama was a 'path until nearly a moon ago."

As if considering this, Tai nodded again. "The Empire is like an overbearing parent; they decide what you should and shouldn't know. Some say it's to protect you, but..."

"But there are those who talk out against them, even in the streets," Mik spoke up, remembering the whispers he'd occasionally heard when Father would take him into Stoneridge on business. "Not everyone believes that the Empire created all good things and brought us out of darkness."

Now it was Soren's turn to snort. "Because raiding Clanfolk are signs of darkness, aye? Soft-bodied Lowlanders." But he grinned at Mikael, who grinned back.

"Better than backward Clanfolk," he said loftily. "Though I'm part Clan too now, so what does that make me?"

Katjin looked thoughtful. "Savior to the Empire and epic hero?" Mikael hoped his bonded was kidding—at least, partly.

When they'd settled down again, Tai began his story. "You know that the Empire came from the south, eh?"

Mikael nodded, remembering what his tutors had taught him over the years. "From the Southern continent. They sailed north and found the Clanfolk and the Highlandfolk."

"And because the Clanfolk thought that the Lowlands were too close to the sea, they weren't too bothered when the Lowlanders settled there," Katjin added. "At least, until the Lowlanders started pressing into the Clan lands. Whether or not it was our fault."

"It was all provoked. We're completely innocent in the matter," was Soren's input. This sounded to Mikael like an old argument, one Katjin and Soren had had many times over the years. "Our raids were in retaliation against them. It wasn't—"

Tai coughed. "The Empire came north, but what most people don't know is that they also came south."

Mikael stared at Tai. Shock stilled all of them, almost making his heart stop. "South?" His voice cracked. "But—"

"The Empire sailed north. They saw the impassible harbors on the northern coasts but pushed forward, trying to find what was on the other side of the mountains," Tai said. Even Mandric looked interested now. "When they got to the other side, they found mostly forest and a narrow bit of lowland that looked suitable for farming."

"So they settled," Mikael said flatly.

Tai nodded. "So they settled. They built a city and they farmed the arable land. But when they ran out of that land, they came to burn our forests. So we stopped them."

Mikael thought about that. "But what about the 'paths? Didn't they do anything about it?"

This time, Tai grinned. "The settlers who went north didn't have 'paths. In fact, they were trying to get away from the 'paths."

Mouth open, Katjin and Soren were both staring at Tai. "No 'paths?" A world without 'paths…

"'Pathing is as much a natural talent for the Empire, as the Shahi's magic is for them. We just both decided to take advantage of what we were blessed with." Tai nodded toward Mandric. "Half-bloods like Mandric mean that there are some 'pathic powers bred into our magics now. So while we might not understand them as much as the Empire, we're probably best able to help the two of you out, especially with our history of dealing with the Empire."

Mikael could feel a knot in his stomach relax, tension

easing that he hadn't even known he was hiding. "So you won't burn the 'pathy out of me? I'll still be a heart-sense?" His hand fumbled for Katjin's, squeezing it tightly. They didn't need to be in constant skin-to-skin contact now, but sometimes it was just nice to have a hand to grip.

Tai's slightly-alien face softened, looked almost gentle. "Katjin's ama was a rare case, and her 'pathy was still latent. We don't want to rid the world of heart-senses and thought-senses. We just want your gifts to be in control, so you can still live with other people."

Tears burned Mik's eyes, and he hiccupped a sob. Not that he'd admit that to Soren, though. Katjin's eyes seemed a little wet too, from what Mikael could see through his blurry eyes. The taste of salt in his mouth wasn't just from his own tears, he could tell that much. Looking up, he noticed both Tai and Mandric's eyes watering up. Starless hells, the crying epidemic could spread to the whole hirhai if he wasn't careful. A couple deep breaths and a ragged bit of tune, and his lungs felt a little more under control. Mandric gave Mikael a brief, tight smile as he swiped at his own eyes.

"So you coexisted with the Empire for a while?" Soren asked, probably trying to divert the attention off the two of them. He'd probably call them 'weeping babes' or something later.

"We did. Once we impressed on them that the forests were ours and the flatlands were theirs, we did. And, while we didn't get along, there were some intermarriages." Tai smiled briefly. "There was even a half-Shahi queen at one point, in what they called the Age of the Black and Gold."

"But then…" Soren prompted, obviously taken by the story. "Then, what happened?"

Tai's face darkened, his shoulders drooping at the memory. "There was plague, and while many of the cityfolk died, few of the Shahi did. So they started to burn our forests. So we retaliated against them."

Tai gave no word about what the retaliation had been, exactly, but Mikael could imagine. It all made sense now, the Cityfolk fleeing back to the Empire and carrying with them tales of Shahi demons.

"So we help whoever it is that flees the Empire." Tai's voice grew fierce. "Because, if it's one more life we can deny the Empire, it will be one more life that lives for the Shahi."

"So you're still fighting them," Mikael said slowly, motivation for the Shahi to take in and protect renegade 'paths suddenly a little clearer. "You never stopped fighting them."

Tai's yellow eyes, fierce in their passion, stared into Mikael's with utmost honestly. "We never stopped," he echoed Mikael's words. "It's why we still do what we can today—anything to undermine the Empire. It's why we'll teach you, so that you can do your part to help."

Mikael exchanged a look with Katjin. Because taking down an Empire was what everyone expected to do after breakfast.

Finally, it came time for Mandric to leave. "I've tarried long enough," he told the three of them, the look on his face regretful. "I need to get back to Nolan, see where we stand."

"It's war then?" Soren asked, his voice flat. Mikael shuddered at the emotions Soren projected: the cold-blooded hate, the anger that he usually suppressed.

A short, sharp nod was Mandric's only acknowledgement. "This may be what brings the Clans down upon the Lowlands, lad," he said in a grave voice. "If something happened to your families—if what we suspect happened—"

"You'll come get us, aye?" Katjin asked, his hand clenching Mikael's so tight that Mik was sure he was losing circulation. "When Apa finds something, you'll come back?"

Mandric put one hand on Katjin's shoulder and one on Soren's, as the three of them stood in a line in front of them. "You know I will, lad." He patted Katjin's cheek. "Keep Tai on his toes. And learn—learn quickly. We need you."

Mikael wasn't sure how much use the three of them would be, but he nodded, just as Kat and Soren did. He tried to swallow around the lump in his throat, but it wasn't working.

At least Mandric smiled at them. "No long faces, eh? I'll be back soon." And with a rough hug for each of them, he shouldered his pack and began the long climb down the trunk of the tree.

"Soon," Soren echoed, as if he was physically clinging to that promise. "Ancestors watch and bless you, Uncle."

"Ancestors bless," Katjin repeated.

"And the stars to guide and the wind at your back," Mikael finished, a feeling of dread growing in his stomach. One more person who had walked into and out of his life; there had to be a point where this would stop. When it was over. When it all was over.

Chapter Three

Apparently Tai decided that a historical retelling of the Empire's relationship with the Shahi was enough for one sitting, so they were left on their own for the afternoon. Soren wanted to go exploring, so they headed out across the hirhai to see what they would find.

"It'll be good for both of you," Soren said at their initial dismissal of the idea. "It'll help little Kat conquer those annoying fears of his, and it'll help you acclimate to being around people again." Then Soren gave him and Katjin what Kat had dubbed 'the sad eyes,' puckering up his lower lip until he looked like he was going to cry.

Katjin shoved Soren in the shoulder as they passed by him.

"Hey!" Soren shouted as Katjin knocked him off balance. "Who saved your arse from the Empire?"

Mikael stuck his tongue out, since it seemed like the right reaction. Katjin snorted. "Remind me next time just to let the Empire get me."

Fingers laced together, Katjin led Mikael out toward the center of the hirhai. "If I think about protecting you and shielding you, then I don't think about... that,"

Katjin muttered, pointing toward the drop-off beyond the wood-and-rope railings that seemed to line every path. "I can't believe I'm walking through a tree."

"Just think of it as city streets," Mikael said, looking up at the canopy above them. "At least we're in the shade." He still wore his peaked Horse Clan hat, to keep the sun off his face. His skin hadn't quite forgiven him for that bad sunburn from his flight out of Stoneridge. Even now, his tan still came in patches and his skin was prone to peeling after prolonged time in the sun. At least he smelled better now. Soren swore it had taken two or three baths, in addition to that first sponging down Katjin had given him, to get the stench of the cellar off. Katjin just gave him a little smile every time he caught Mikael frantically washing his hands. Mikael thought he caught of whiff of that fetid air every once in a while. Then again, reminding Katjin of Mikael's own fears seemed to ease Katjin's anxiety as well.

That seemed to help Katjin a little bit. The branch that they walked on was about a stride and a half wide, meaning that two people could pass each other without knocking anyone over. All the Shahi seemed to be small and slim, with abnormally long fingers. Mik wondered if living in trees for generations had anything to do with that. Soren's bulk loomed even larger out here, especially in the small space inside their hirh.

Branch pathways looped over and under theirs, occasionally coming to a forced crossroads where someone had thoughtfully built a platform to connect the two. The hirhai itself was situated in a circle around what looked to be some kind of clearing, two or three hirh to a tree and all sorts of ladders and paths connecting in-between. Smoke curling out of a stone chimney and a large beehive oven marked the baker's, and anyone with a nose could find the tannery, placed on the exact opposite end of the hirhai as their little hirh. Children seemed confined to one or two platforms, circled around adults that seemed to be leading them in some kind of teaching song. It was strange to hear the sounds of life surrounding them again: a distant hammer from what was probably the forge, the staccato beat of an axe as it chopped wood somewhere, the high voices of the children as they chattered through their lessons. He hadn't realized how lonely he'd been—how lonely they'd all been—with just the three of them for company.

"There's no rhythm," Kat said suddenly, his hand tightening around Mikael's. Mik felt a little self-conscious, walking hand-in-hand like a child through this village. Adults didn't hold hands like this, as if they were afraid of losing each other, but there wasn't much he could do about that.

"What?" It took a minute for Katjin's comment to register. "No rhythm—"

When he listened, and listened closely, it was true. Every motion seemed to be off-beat. Footsteps didn't seem to have any discernable pattern to them, and the person chopping wood seemed to pause in a random fashion, as if they were afraid of falling into a rhythm. Only the sounds of the children's voices seemed to have any predictable measurement to it.

"Maybe they're afraid of patterns?" Soren asked, his own eyes wide. "Maybe it's part of their beliefs, that the demons will get them if they fall into rhythm? Tai kept saying things about the earth energies. Maybe patterns release those demon spirits."

"Apa's mentioned stranger things," Katjin added.

"The fisherfolk on the coast would always buy headscarves by the wagon-load, because they thought that it would protect their minds from being read by the thought-senses."

Mikael snorted. "What kind of backward person believes that?"

Katjin shrugged. "Just because it sounds strange to us doesn't mean it they can't believe it sounds perfectly logical."

"Maybe their ancestors don't like rhythm," Soren said. "Meke always told me that ours didn't like loud noises after dark." At Katjin's grin, Soren scowled. "What?"

Then it occurred to Mikael. "Remember Tai? How he got angry when Kat started tapping?"

Soren shrugged. "They eat babies for breakfast. I swear I saw some grated up in the porridge."

They ventured further into the hirhai. The rush of emotions got stronger, the further they went in. Each emotion washed over him like a wave: irritation at having to listen to this lesson again, the pain of trying to hammer a broken rail back in place to prevent another baby from diving off the edge, annoyance and happiness and everything in between. He tried to block the negative emotions, ignoring anything that made his gut twist. Instead, he tried to focus on the happy emotions, one in particular that grabbed his attention. He blushed. Someone in the hirh was obviously having a... happily productive day, if the sudden tightness in his leggings were any evidence of that.

Next to him, Katjin squirmed a little. Mikael grinned at him, tugging at Katjin's hand, wiggling his eyebrows. Katjin laughed out loud, which was the final thing Mikael needed to drive all those bad feelings away.

"You too?" Katjin asked, blushing slightly. "Ancestors damn it, I knew that whole blood-bond was a bad idea."

Soren looked back and forth between the two of them, as if he was trying to figure out their secret. "Oh, ancestors!" he burst out. "Do I need to dunk the two of you into another pond?"

Their laughter seemed to attract some attention—unwanted as it was. The hirhai went silent the minute they started laughing. The laughter built and built until Mikael's sides hurt, and tears streamed down his face. It swelled out of him and up into the trees until it seemed like the very trees were laughing. Both Katjin and Soren clutched at their sides, looking hysterical. The expression seemed to be mirrored on the faces that peered out at them from the hirhai windows all around them. Mikael rubbed at his watery eyes to get a better look.

They were all laughing. In their laughter, though, was fear, as if they didn't know why they were laughing.

Starless hells.

Mikael stopped, Without realizing it, they had made it to the village center now, a platform almost one hundred strides or more in diameter. In one corner, a group of fellas about Soren's age were doing some kind of military drill, but they'd stopped as soon as they heard the three of them. Even the children at their lessons, a couple trees back, were looking down at them. It wasn't with curiosity though, it was with fear.

"Katjin, stop!" He pinched at Katjin, who yelped.

"What you do that for?" Katjin asked, a rush of welcomed irritation buzzing around him. "What—"

Mikael pointed to the now quiet Shahi, most of whom looked relieved and not at all comfortable at the fact that the three of them stood at the center of their hirhai.

"Um, hi?" Katjin said, waving his free hand at everyone.

Soren snorted. "Nice job, fellas," he muttered, socking both Katjin and Mikael in the shoulder. Even Soren looked uneasy. "I thought you weren't going to do that anymore."

"Wasn't like I was trying," Mikael said in a low voice. "It could've been worse, though."

"At least Kat didn't start singing," Soren said, obviously trying to lighten the mood. Mikael felt grateful. This was one more side-effect of his 'pathy that he really didn't want to think about. He appreciated Soren trying to take their minds off of it. "Then they'd leave us for those moah-bird monsters we heard last night."

"Kat would probably scare the moah away," Mikael retorted before noticing Kat's narrowed eyes and pursed lips. It didn't take a 'path to know that Katjin was getting angry, and an angry Kat meant that his own emotions were about to get more out of whack than they already were.

"Easy," he soothed, his free hand rubbing Katjin's shoulder. "Y'know we don't mean anything by it."

"Not like I don't know I can't sing," Katjin muttered darkly. "You don't have to rub it in."

Well-aware that all eyes were on them now, and that fear and curiosity seemed to be the dominant emotions, Mikael freed his hand from Katjin and put both hands on Kat's shoulders. "Hey," he said softly, the weight of all those glances almost physically resting on his shoulders. "Doesn't matter how well you sing, or even if you can. Your song saved me, remember?" He thought he was dead when he heard that song, that off-key voice the sweetest thing in the world at that moment. "You. Saved me. Because you sang to me."

Katjin's sullen look lifted, though his eyes remained downcast at the wooden planks. "Really?" He sounded skeptical.

Trying to ignore the pain and the doubt, Mikael brought Katjin into a quick, tight hug. "Aye, dummy. And if I have to get Soren to beat it into your thick skull, I will."

Katjin sniffled against his shoulder. "Just as long as he does it offbeat," his bonded said. "Don't want to get Tai even more mad at us. He might move creepy Aidan in with us as punishment."

Mikael couldn't help laughing at that. And as much as he really wanted to kiss Katjin in front of all these people—his beautiful, bright, happy Katjin—he knew that would be pushing it. While the Empire didn't really seem to care who you kissed or cuddled or—dare he even think about it—lay with, starless hells knew what the Shahi would think.

"Two sniffle-fests in one day," Soren said, coming up to clasp them both by the shoulder. "I think all that time alone turned you into a bunch of girls." Three moons ago, Mikael knew that Katjin would've slugged his cousin. Now, Kat just grabbed Soren and dragged him into the impromptu hug instead.

Soren ducked out of the hug and ran back toward the hirh as fast as he could. "Now you have to catch me!" he called out gleefully.

"You're sure he's the adult here?" Mikael asked Katjin, dubious about it all.

Katjin smirked. "You'd think. And no one ever brings up the night he and his friends decided to try Febe's not-quite-ready aisrag and how sick it made them all for days."

Snorting with laughter, Mikael grabbed Katjin's hand and took off after Soren. "We can catch him," he yelled as they ran. "He's not that fast!"

They flew across the narrow branches, dodging and ducking tree limbs. As they rounded the corner of the trunk closest to their hirh, Mikael felt his robe catch on a wayward branch. He pitched toward the rail-less edge of the tree branch, his head suddenly facing the ground. He scrabbled for an edge to catch, but only got Katjin instead.

"Kat—" he moaned, closing his eyes. Their heads would squish like fruit, their brains—

Except they didn't hit.

Mikael opened his eyes. Tai stood on a limb just lengths from them, his arms reaching out as if to grab them. His eyes were closed, sweat dripping down his face as he *strained*. Then Mikael looked down, and realized that Tai had stopped them in midair.

"Ancestors—" Katjin started flailing next to him, legs swimming frantically, trying to catch at something. "Soren!" he shrieked.

"Damn it, Kat!" was Soren's response, panicked as he threw a rope down to them. "Grab it, quick! Tai can't hold you for much longer."

Mikael grabbed at the rope, holding on for dear life. Just as his hands closed around it and he wrapped his legs around it for good measure, he could feel the spell give. They fell another stride, and Mikael's left leg slammed into the tree trunk. He hissed in pain.

"You okay?" Katjin's green eyes were wider than Mikael had ever seen them, the whites showing clearly around the green irises. "Ancestors help us…" he moaned.

"I'm going to pass out."

"No, you're not," Mikael grunted, getting a better grip on Katjin's arms. "You can pull us up now," he yelled at Soren. "Please?"

The haul up seemed almost as long and arduous as that first time they'd come up the trees. Katjin seemed to waver in and out of consciousness, arms wrapped so tight around Mikael that Mikael thought his breathing was going to be cut off. By the time they got back to the safety of the platform, all Mikael wanted to do was cling to the solid wooden planks under him, swearing he'd never leave them again.

"Thank you," he panted toward Tai. Tai looked as pale as Katjin.

"We do save people on occasion," Tai said, wobbling to his feet. "Not just eating babies." And before Mikael could say anything else, the Shahi disappeared.

"That was magic," Soren said quietly, untangling them from the rope. "And Aidan's supposed to be even more powerful?"

That was something Mikael didn't even want to think about.

"We've got to find something to do," Soren said, laying on his back on their platform. They were all looking up at the sunlight that filtered through the trees. After lunch, it had rained for about two sun-spans, or what they could estimate as a span, since you couldn't exactly track the sun through all the trees. "What if we head down to the floor?"

Mikael rolled over to face Soren, arching an eyebrow

at him. "And you propose us getting down there how?"

"And back up," Katjin added. He shuddered. "I really don't want to go up in one of those baskets again."

"Well, if you two could separate for more than a few seconds," Soren muttered. "Hey! We could practice that. I mean, you two were separated for an entire day when the Empire—" He stopped, as if he noticed how pale Mikael suddenly felt. "But you were separated for an entire day, and that didn't kill you," he finished. The guilt Soren felt was obvious, which made Mikael feel a little more considerate toward him—a little more forgiving too, at least this time.

"There's all those walkways," Mikael said slowly, eyeing the number of wooden paths that veered off from their platform. "If we can find a ladder, we could practice on that."

"And if they train their scouts or military at all, they should have some kind of grounds somewhere," Soren added, probably remembering that group that had been training. When Mikael thought about it, he thought he'd seen both men and women there. The Empire's cavalry was mostly comprised of men, just because it was the men that the Clanfolk sent off to be soldiers. 'Paths were both male and female, though they weren't always proficient in any sort of protective arts, as he'd seen first-hand in the cavalry camp.

"We could ask Tai," Katjin said, still sounding unconvinced.

Mikael shook Katjin lightly. "C'mon, Kat, we have to try sometime. Do you really want to go through life constantly tied together like this?"

When Katjin didn't say anything, Mikael closed his eyes and groaned. For all his brilliance, Katjin seemed to have problems with self-esteem every now and then. He couldn't get through his thick head that he was a more-than-adequate son of the plains, and a wonderful person in general. Of course, the events of the past few moons wouldn't exactly help anyone's outlook. As much as Mikael wanted to have Katjin there to protect him every moment of every day, he did realize that he would need to go off by himself at some point. It would also be awfully nice to do his business without an audience someday.

"C'mon," he repeated, dragging Katjin to his feet. "I'm doing this for both of us." Before Katjin could say anything, he held up his hand. "I'm not doing this to break the bond. I'm doing it to strengthen it." Behind Katjin, Soren nodded vigorously in agreement. "Because if we ever get separated again, we can't go through life drugged out of our brains. We have to be able to function."

"I guess, especially when we do go back," Katjin said slowly, grudgingly. His green eyes seemed to search Mikael's very soul, looking very young. "You're sure you don't want to break the bond?"

Mikael shook his head frantically. "Never," he said, putting every ounce of emphasis into it that he could. "Never, Kat. I know we're stuck together, and I want that. I just... I want to be prepared, aye?"

They knew it would happen. It was inevitable that the Empire would try to take down one or both of them, preferably both. While he tried not to think about what life would be without Katjin, his light, he knew he had to prepare for it in any case. Just because.

Katjin finally nodded. "Let's go."

They found a platform a few trees over from theirs, a neglected practice platform of some kind from the look of it. Covered cabinets were built into the trunk of the tree, storing wooden knives and swords. One raised plank spanned the right side of the platform, a series of blocks and other obstacles ringing the other. A ladder went up six feet before it connected to a smaller platform above, a rope hanging back down to the platform they were on.

Soren surveyed the area, looking satisfied with what he found. "This should do." He crossed his arms, then turned to look back at Mikael and Katjin. "Okay, up the ladder."

Mikael and Katjin both stared at him. Then they turned to each other. "We got up and down the ladder in the hirh," Katjin said, his voice doubtful. "If you go up, and then I follow and keep one hand on your ankle."

"Or if you go up and I follow right behind you, back to front," Mikael offered, squinting at the ladder. "My arms should reach around you, especially if I—" He demonstrated, pinning Katjin's body to the ladder and using his longer arms to grab at the ladder rungs. Except doing that caused other… problems that probably wouldn't help them get up the ladder any sooner. At least the blood bond was satisfied by touching through clothes; as long as they could feel body heat, the pain stayed manageable.

Soren coughed. "Or you could just go up the ladder." He'd found a very long stick somewhere, almost two strides in length. Holding the stick in one hand, he hit the palm of his other hand with it, making a twhapping noise. Mikael suddenly had a very bad feeling about all of this.

"Soren—" Katjin started, but then found the stick descending toward him. Soren hit Kat with it squarely on the arse. "What the hell are you doing?" Kat yelled. "You stupid—"

"Up the ladder!" Soren barked, the stick descending again.

Katjin scrambled up the ladder, Mikael close behind him. Once they were perched on the higher platform, they stared down at Soren and panted. Soren just grinned at them.

"There, was that so hard?" Soren asked cheekily, twirling his stick. "Now, come back down."

Katjin shook his head emphatically. "Not til you lose the stick."

Mikael could hear Soren growling under his breath, even from three lengths above Soren's head. "Damn it, Kat, just get your arse down here." He waved the stick again.

Katjin's eyes met Mikael's. For once, Mik completely supported Katjin's continual annoyance at Soren. "On three," Mik said quietly. "One, two—"

As one, they launched themselves off the platform, tackling Soren to the ground. While Katjin sat on Soren's chest, Mikael wrenched the stick out of Soren's hand and tossed it off the platform. "Take that!" Mikael said, poking Soren in the ribs. "You and your damned stick."

The sound of laughter echoed behind them. Mikael turned around quickly, only to find Aidan staring at them, laughing hysterically.

"Ha ha," Mikael said, blushing fiercely. The last thing he needed was the Shahi boy finding them funny. That very thought annoyed him almost as much as Soren's breathing annoyed Katjin.

"Da wants," Aidan said, once he'd stopped laughing. He pointed at Katjin and Mikael. "Wants you. Aye?"

Mikael still wasn't too sure what think about Tai. He seemed nice enough—for a Shahi—but the way Tai looked at him, almost hungrily, bothered Mikael. Yesterday evening, after dinner, Tai had spent close to a hand span quizzing Mikael on how everyone was feeling, and what his range was. As if he would know what his own range was, especially after being isolated from anyone. He hadn't exactly strolled down a city street anytime recently, and for his entire stay in Katjin's grandparents' camp, he'd been unconscious. The questions had been a little too probing, the light in Tai's strange yellow eyes a little too feverish for his taste. Especially considering the snatches of conversation they heard, what sounded like some kind of reports on people moving throughout the Highlands and plains—it all made Mikael wonder if there was more going on, as if they'd accidentally fallen into a plot to undermine the Empire. It wasn't that he minded, exactly, since that was his eventual aim, but it would've been nice if they asked first.

Looking at Katjin, Mikael shrugged. "I suppose we have to go?" He didn't bother hiding the doubt in his voice. Katjin would've picked up on the emotion anyway.

Soren got the hint as well. "Maybe I'll go too," he said, herding Katjin and Mikael back to the main platform, this time without his stick. "Might as well hear what the demon-man has to say."

Aidan led them up to the platform in front of their hirh. Tai sat there, waiting for them.

"Aye?" Katjin asked, putting on what Mikael recognized as his 'polite face.' While not quite the picture of innocence, it would probably fool anyone who wasn't a 'path—or who didn't know Kat.

"Sit down." Tai patted the platform in front of him. "I just had a few questions."

Mikael groaned. He could already guess where this

was going.

They sat side by side, all three in a line. Sandwiched in protectively between Soren and Katjin, Mikael couldn't help feeling a little more secure than he had in a while. While Soren's touch and presence still got to be a little too much sometimes—sensory overload, Mandric had called it—the older boy's bulk was still a welcome addition. He still wondered, sometimes, who was protecting whom, though.

Tai stared at them for a while, as if considering them. Even as Mikael squirmed under the heaviness of that gaze, Katjin started tapping his fingers against the wooden plank floor of the platform.

Ta-Tap. Ta-Tap. Ta-Ta-Ta-Tap. Ta—

"Ow!" Katjin howled, waving his red, swelling fingers. "What was that for?"

Mikael grabbed at Soren, preventing him from jumping up and strangling the Shahi. Even Aidan looked startled.

"Rhythm," Tai hissed. "There will be no rhythm within the hirhai, understand?"

"What's wrong with rhythm?" Katjin asked, examining his wounded fingers.

Tai at least looked apologetic for thwaping Kat, though Mikael had to resist the urge to thwap the man back. "Rhythmic beats are what we use to concentrate to call the energy from the magic lines," he said, looking sheepish. "We probably should've told you about that ahead of time."

"Probably," Soren snorted. "You're lucky that the amazing duo over here didn't already blow anything up—not that they won't. Trouble seems to stick to Kat, especially, like a burr."

A nod from Tai. "Legend says it goes back to one of

our greatest queens and her tendency to explode anything she was trying to change. It just became easier to limit any unnatural pattern to ritual. We don't think twice about it anymore, since it's the way we're taught, but to outsiders…"

"It's meditation," Mikael said. "'Paths use something like that to control their powers, don't they?" The 'paths in the Empire camp had spent most of the time to themselves, sequestered in their tent away from everyone. Even when he'd been imprisoned in there, with them, they hadn't done much more than stare at their hands or at the wall in silence.

Again, Tai nodded. "Some people can easily control the magic, shaping it to their will. Others need help, so we use the song-lines—the spells—to tell the magic where to go. Song-lines can be just songs, or they can involve dances, depending on how delicate or complicated the spell is. When a child beats out something in rhythm, it can awake power that they don't necessarily mean to cause."

"Your… scouts? They drill in unison. Doesn't that stir up all the magical whatsit?" Soren asked, his hands folded neatly in his lap.

"All the drills our scouts do are off-beat. There is a pattern, but it's broken out into passes that don't necessarily share the same number of movements or in an equal direction. And since they learn it by rote…"

Soren looked pleased at this. "Can we see?" he asked, excitement building around him like a cloud of nervous energy.

Tai considered this. "We can have someone show you the atah-atah—the shadow dance," he said. "It might help you fit into our routine of life a bit more."

"Just not the rhythm of it," Katjin said, sounding sour at a chance to learn and fail at yet another self-defense drill. "What is the atah-atah?" He stumbled over the unfamiliar word. "This shadow dancing thing, is it weapon-fighting?"

"It's what it sounds like—solitary weapons training, where you battle your own shadow rather than someone else. There are two sequences of moves, so it can be performed as a mirror action—atah-atah, self with self—and each sequence is a reaction to the other. It can be done with a shortsword and a knife or paired long knives," Tai said, moving over toward the cabinet that seemed built into the trunk of the tree. He opened it, pulling out a pair of long wooden knives. "There are twelve passes, and each pass has its offensive and defensive stance." He demonstrated a defensive stance, his left foot perpendicular to his right foot, arms above his head and knives pointing forward in what looked to Mikael like the high guard his sword master had taught him.

They watched Tai move through pass after pass of knife play that almost seemed like a dance. It was true that there was no discernable rhythm or pattern to it, though each thrust and block seemed to flow one into the next.

"It is logical, if you look at it as a whole," Soren said, his eyes completely focused on Tai's weaving body and knives. "Especially if you tie the defensive to the offensive."

Katjin seemed a little less interested, but from everything that Kat and Soren had told him, Kat had never been the best at weapons practice. He was obviously adequate, since he had survived years of practicing with Soren, but Mikael knew that Kat felt more than a little inadequate now.

"We could probably set you up with someone to show you the basics," Tai said, as if he didn't expect them to master it. Mikael only hoped that Soren would prove them wrong.

"Father, I?" a voice from behind them spoke up. Mikael looked behind him to find Aidan standing there, a long knife in each hand. "I."

Tai said something in Shahi, which Aidan answered in short, biting remarks.

"My son has offered to teach you," he said, waving a hand toward Aidan. "He does need the practice, and it may help to increase the boundaries of your range." This, he obviously aimed at Mikael and Katjin.

Mikael looked at Katjin, who was scuffing his toe on the plank floor. "Do we have to be good at it?" he asked, for Katjin's sake.

A smile creased Tai's face. "It isn't something your life will depend on."

Soren was champing at the bit, ready to steal the knives from Tai's hands at that very moment to begin. Katjin still hung back, unsure. Mikael himself couldn't decide if he was vibrating because Soren was fidgety, or because Katjin was strung tighter than a wire. He could only do so much, though, and it wasn't as if he could mind Katjin's moods every second of the day.

"I'll try," he said, freeing his hand gently from Katjin's and reaching for the two knives that Tai held out. Though they were made out of wood, the balance on each blade was still amazing, the weight feeling just right in his hands. "It's been moons since I've held anything with an edge, so—"

Aidan jumped in, attacking with his blades. Mikael automatically put out his palms, deflecting Aidan's wrists and using Aidan's own movement to steer him in the opposite direction. The Shahi looked impressed, as did Aidan's father.

"Not bad, Lowlander," Tai said, a new respect in his voice. "You may be a credit to the Empire yet, if you survive the journey home."

Tai's next words didn't register though, because Aidan was approaching with another attack. This time, Mikael corrected his grip on the hilts of the knives and was able to parry the attack. He went into high stance, catching Aidan's diagonal cut that was aimed at his chest as he slid into hanging guard. It wasn't quite the same as fighting with a short sword and dagger in his off-hand, but he was holding his own.

Time seemed to blur as he and Aidan danced around each other. He could feel the anticipation building, the excitement bubbling up in his opponent that seemed to drive Aidan faster and faster. Mikael gripped that emotion, holding onto it with everything it had and letting it push him to his limits. He watched Aidan's body, trying to predict Aidan's next move through the muscle cues. He could almost sense and anticipate the next strike, as if the adrenaline pushing Aidan's body was cueing his own.

He finally heard Tai call "Halt!" He automatically fell back into guard, ready for the next pass. "Easy, lads."

Mikael blinked sweat out of his eyes, suddenly aware that both Soren and Katjin were staring at him. Soren grinned, his pride obvious even from the other side of the platform. Katjin, though…

Katjin was a reeling ball of misery, conflicted between pride at his bonded and the utmost betrayal, because Mikael proved good at something Katjin had always failed miserably at. Before Mik could go to Kat, though,

Aidan intercepted him with a cry of congratulations, and a fighter's embrace. Mikael's body froze, and he automatically pushed the other boy away. Aidan looked hurt, but before Mikael could do anything to counteract that, Soren had swept him up into a back-beating hug of his own.

After being pounded on the back by Soren, Mikael turned to find Katjin. His bonded had somehow escaped off the platform, and Mikael's body was now well-aware of that fact as the adrenaline wore off.

"Where is he?" he panted, shading his eyes with his hand. The dappled light that filtered through the trees still blasted as bright as bare noon sun, though, and he could see spots through his closed lids. The nausea would start at any minute, since the headache had obviously arrived. "Katjin."

He heard Soren mutter something about spoiled babies and the thunder of footsteps as Soren ran off down one of the walkways. Aidan's hand pressed insistently on Mikael's shoulders, urging him to sit down. A waterskin was shoved in his hands, and Tai's voice commanded, "Drink, Mikael."

He drank, letting the sweet fruit juice slide down his throat. He could feel some of the energy returning, but his head still ached something fierce. "Where's Kat?" he repeated, his voice choking in his throat now.

"Fight it," Tai said. "Concentrate, just like you were doing with Aidan. Focus on the emotion, not the lack. Concentrate and let it pass over you, not consume you."

Tai, looking around to probably see if anyone was listening, began surreptitiously tapping out a rhythm, a beat that Mikael knew. He started to hum the tune that went along with the rhythm, forcing himself to get out every bar that he knew. He took the music in, focusing on it so much that it became the beat of his heart, the breath that he took in and out, the rush of blood behind his eyes.

His pounding heart slowed, and the spots behind his eyes seemed to dim. He could hear more than just the blood rushing through his ears now, and the world seemed to settle on its axis again. He concentrated, trying harder and harder to force the world into what it should be—still.

Voices came from nearby, Soren's deeper one and Katjin's still-treble, cracking with every other word. Footsteps flew toward him, and Mikael groped blindly for the arms that he knew would be there. Lips touched his cheek, his neck, his nose, whatever they could reach. He settled down into that embrace, because he knew it was where he belonged.

Even if he had forgotten for a little while.

Tai gave them a speculative look as they settled back at the practice platform that afternoon, backs against the padded, waist-high wooden rails. "Katjin," he said slowly, "can you explain exactly how you shield Mikael?"

Katjin was suspicious, that much was obvious, especially the way his fingers kept plucking at the embroidered trim on his robe and how he kept avoiding Tai's eyes. "I step in front of him. Sometimes physically, sometimes I just imagine myself doing it. And if there's a bad emotion coming, I deflect it."

The Shahi nodded, as if considering something. "Do you actually visualize bouncing the emotion off of you?"

Mikael wanted to protest, because emotions couldn't be seen as physical things. They had physical results, aye, but not an actual physical shape. They caused his body to react, for either good or bad, but it wasn't like anger was blue and furry or joy was green and smooth.

Even Katjin seemed a little taken back by the question. "No, I just push it away."

In those first days, Katjin had kept Mikael behind him, physically acting as a shield. Once they got better at reading each other and the emotions around them, though, neither of them had to physically lead to shield, especially since there was the occasional spillover that Mikael knew Katjin didn't deserve to feel.

"But you feel the emotions, just like a heart-sense does," Tai persisted, leaning closer to Katjin. "You can see them the same way Mikael does."

Katjin pushed back, panic feeding through his link to Mikael. Mikael fought the urge to grab Katjin and run, wondering why Tai kept pressing the issue. "The blood bond made him a heart-sense," Mikael snapped. "He feels what I feel, he senses what I sense. Sometimes he feels something before I do, and if he needs to, he protects me from it. He filters out the emotions I don't need."

"Straining, filtering, funneling." Tai mused over something. There was no malice that Mikael could sense in him, but he didn't feel like trusting the man. Tai seemed a little too interested in exactly how their bond worked for Mikael's taste, especially since the memory of what happened to Katjin's ama was all too present in both their minds.

"Does it make a difference how he does it?" Mikael asked. "We don't care about that part. We just care about this." He held up their joined hands. "We'll keep the bond. We just don't want to be in physical contact all the time."

A shudder went through Katjin's body. As the guilt and rejection seemed to spool tighter and tighter through Katjin, Mikael sent the most soothing thoughts of reassurance that he could. Damn it, he didn't want to break the two of them off. He just wanted to be able to do things by himself again, be useful again.

Tai was studying them again, eyes going back and forth between them as if he was trying to read them somehow. Mandric had assured them that Tai wasn't a 'path, but Mikael wondered sometimes, especially since all his instincts told him not to completely trust the Shahi.

"Meditations might help," Tai said finally. "When Mikael fenced with Aidan, the physical limitations didn't seem to bother him." He looked directly at Mik. "Did they?"

Mikael shook his head. "I didn't notice it," he admitted. "I guess I was caught up in the moment."

Then Tai turned to Katjin. "When you rescued Mikael, how did you manage the separation?"

Katjin blushed slightly. "Aisrag," he admitted. "And some brew that Mandric gave Soren. Some relaxant. Those and the adrenaline seemed to take my mind off the pain."

"But he slept for days after," Mikael added. The weariness had dragged at him, too, for a few days afterward.

Tai nodded. "I don't want to resort to any potions," he said to himself. "Meditation. Endurance. Keeping the mind occupied."

Mikael exchanged a look with Katjin, who shrugged. Tai shook himself slightly, as if he remembered where he was and who he was with.

"Meditation, lads," he said. "We're going to learn to quiet the mind. Let's try this one."

He had them sit cross-legged on two large cushions. They sat back to back, to keep the bond satisfied at their physical proximity. When Tai brought out blindfolds and what looked like furry ear muffs for them, though, Mikael drew the line.

"Absolutely not," he said. "No dark. I don't care what you say or do to me. I will not wear that." He could still taste the dirty gag the cavalry 'paths had shoved in his mouth to keep him quiet. And the blindfold—if they wanted another incident like at the Highlandfolk camp, they'd get one as soon as they look away his ability to see. "I can close my eyes just fine, thank you."

Before Tai could protest, Soren growled. "Might as well do what he says. Probably better if they're cooperating instead of forcing. Unless you Shahi really are as sadistic as the stories say."

Tai took a deep breath, and then put the blindfolds and ear muffs away. "Okay, no blindfolds. You need to keep your eyes closed, though," he said, waving a finger at them warningly. "And you—" he pointed at Soren, "you need to keep complete silence."

Soren only smirked before settling back against the railing in a more comfortable position. "Do I get a cushion too?"

Ignoring that last remark, Tai turned back to Katjin and Mikael. "Okay, close your eyes. I want you to concentrate on my voice."

Mikael closed his eyes, watching the play of light against the backs of his eyelids. It was so much easier, knowing that all he had to do was open his eyes to find the light again. Too much darkness brought too much anxiety, and then his lungs seized up and he couldn't breathe.

"No thinking," Tai's voice said. "Breathe in and out. Fill your belly with air. Collect the air into a ball in your belly and hold it there. Let the air out, pushing it out through your belly, up through your lunds and into the air."

Mikael inhaled, feeling Katjin's back muscles contracting as his bonded did the same thing. He held the air in, not sure how exactly to collect the air into a ball in his belly, but he did it. He could feel his stomach straining in an attempt to take in more air.

Then, the exhale. He released his breath into the air, slumping back against Katjin as he did so.

"Take it in," Tai droned on. "Take in the green, take in the peace. Take in the calm."

The air was sharp and cool and wet, moistening his nasal passages. The air tasted alive, spicy. He almost didn't want to release it, stale as it was becoming.

"Breathe out the bad, the black, the noxious. Breathe out the hate, the pain."

In with the good, out with the bad. As Tai's voice went on and on, Mikael felt himself slipping into the pattern of the breathing. He tried to bring in the calm, forcing out the anxiety of the past moons. He remembered the quiet of their valley, the peace of the stream and just listening to the water flow. He felt the weight of the trees, looking down on him and his short little life, taking in the air that they'd breathed off for centuries even before the Empire had been born.

"And stand."

Mikael struggled to his feet. He rose, trying not to lose

the pattern of his breathing. He felt Katjin's warmth at his back, their bodies moving in tandem as they breathed in and out as one.

"And sit."

Tai repeated that until the very motions seemed to blur in Mikael's mind. All he knew was the sound of his own breathing and the feeling of the cold air entering his lungs and filling his belly. All he knew was peace.

"Open your eyes."

Mikael stared at Tai, the rush of emotion suddenly flooding his system again in a riot of color and light.

"Breathe, Mikael. Use your breathing to keep it at bay." Tai's voice was low, soothing.

A snore rumbled from behind them. Mikael turned to look over his shoulder, not surprised to find Soren, slumped against the rail, fast asleep.

"Did it work?" Katjin asked, his voice muzzy.

Tai actually smiled at them—a small smile, but still a smile. "I think it worked. We'll have to explore more of this."

So it went for days. They got up. Tai or Aidan brought them breakfast and then herded them outside. Soren went off to drill with the other scouts, while Mikael and Katjin went through exercise after exercise. They meditated. Tai had them focus on one sound or smell, or a range of sounds or smells, then on finding individual emotions—except any sort of randy behavior. Tai seemed somewhat reluctant to deal with the more…base instincts of the body. They shadowed each other through sword and stick drills. Tai even tested them for any magic potential, just out of curiosity.

"I want you to close your eyes," he began, sitting them on the familiar cushions. Katjin groaned. "It's not meditation today," Tai continued, with more humor than usual evident in his voice. "Today, we're going to find magic."

"I think Apa would disown me," Katjin muttered. "It's one thing, binding yourself to a 'path. It's another if you actually come home with a Shahi demon."

Mikael choked back a laugh. He couldn't help imagining the looks on Mandric's and Apa's faces as they rode into the Highland camp, trailing Aidan like a puppy behind them. "Maybe if we brought a moah bird—"

"A-hem," Tai coughed. "If you'd close your eyes..."

With slow sighs, they both complied.

"Now, I want you to cast yourself out," Tai said softly. "Remember what we did yesterday, trying to find that sorrow?"

Eyes closed, Mikael nodded. It had been a young girl, trapped when her foot got caught in a branch about a hundred lengths from the hirhai.

"Good. This time..." Tai hesitated. "This time, I want you to find something else. Something that feels like fire."

Mikael jerked his head, eyes flying open. "What?"

Tai snapped his fingers at Mik. "Eyes closed," he commanded. "Breathe in and out. Fill your belly. Find the warmth."

Air in, held in the belly, expelled out; Mikael let the silent rhythm of his breathing calm his pounding heart. Even Katjin, at his back, seemed to relax, leaning into their tandem breathing. Mikael sent his awareness in all directions, trying, as Tai had told them, to find whatever this 'warmth' was that Tai was talking about. He'd gotten a lot better at picking out individual emotions—especially after Tai threatened to hit him with a stick if he didn't *focus*—and at blocking the extraneous ones. He ignored the usual tiredness and boredom, loneliness and doldrums that seemed to plague the hirhai on an everday basis and attempted to pick up on this mystical 'warmth.'

He tried. He honestly did. There was a bit of warmth, but that had just been two teenagers, apparently taking advantage of an empty hirh for an afternoon rut. There was a shout of triumph from Soren, lengths and lengths away and the rush of blood that usually came from a successful kill on a hunt. But warmth? That buzzing, twitching feeling that made his hair stand on end during lightning storms?

Nothing.

He opened an eye, not surprised to find Tai staring at him intently.

"Anything?" Tai's voice was hopeful.

Mikael shook his head. "Unless Kat…"

"Nothing." Mik was almost overwhelmed by the sense of Katjin's relief. "What now?"

Tai only sighed. "I suppose that's the end of lessons for now. You're coming along well." And with that, the Shahi abruptly left the platform, wandering off to wherever he went.

"He's not related to Mandric, is he?" Mikael asked, wondering if the strangeness ran in the blood.

Katjin laughed in response.

It was raining again. That didn't mean that they were exempt from training, though. Tai had them out in the rain, stumbling over and under and around any branches that fell on the path Tai led them through.

Mikael couldn't pick out any signs marking it as a trail. It seemed as if they were randomly scrambling up and down tree trunks, only some of which actually had the rope-and-wood-ladders that the Shahi were so fond of. The three of them—Soren included—were roped together, at least, and Tai carried that blasted stick of his, ready to poke and prod and re-balance one of them as necessary. That still didn't help the occasional feeling of dizziness that came over Mikael. The thick, intertwining branches below them, at least, obscured how far down the ground was, and the pungeant scent of sappy leaves crushed beneath their feet actually distracted him a little. It reminded him of those damned potions Soren shoved down his throat, those first few days at the camp in the valley. As long as he concentrated on that, he wouldn't try and look.

Down.

Katjin rammed into his back. Mikael thrashed a bit, grabbing wildly at the branches that hung just above his head. Soren often had to duck an overhanging branch, but now, Mikael was just glad he had something to grip to regain his balance.

"Damn it, Kat, do you have your eyes closed or something?" Normally, he wouldn't take his anger out at Katjin. Normally, he wouldn't be prowling through wet, steamy trees in sloshing boots and a tunic that hadn't been any drier than 'damp' in more than a moonspan.

"Maybe I do. What's wrong with that?" Katjin countered. Sure enough, when Mik looked over his shoulder, Katjin's eyes were tightly shut. "If I can't see the ground, I can't know how far it is down."

"Forty lengths," Tai spoke up helpfully. "A fall from this height would kill you. Is that a problem?"

The anger built, burning at Mikael's insides. He was bruised, he was battered, and darkest night, but he never wanted to see another tree in his life.

If he could find those stupid magic lines, he'd definitely burn the forest down. Just to finally be dry.

"That is a problem." Mikael strode forward, dragging Katjin and Soren along behind him. "Why? Because this isn't helping us any, and it sure as starless hells isn't bringing down that stupid Empire you hate so much!" He poked Tai in the chest with his forefinger. "You never tell us anything, you order us around like we're your soldiers—or your son—and it's not helping us any!"

The anger built. Katjin fueled it, his frustration fanning the flames higher and higher. Soren added extra kindling, with his fatigue at the endless patrols around the hirhai, the lack of any action, the sense of sitting on his hands while something—anything could be happening at home.

"Damn it, Tai!" The air began to grow warm. "Don't you see? You're not doing anything!" The trees around him began to waver, the air steam until he couldn't see anything but white vapor. "Damn it!"

"Tai?" He could hear voices from far off, someone shouting at him. Hands that felt like Katjin's clutched at him, only adding to the fire. Mikael held his breath, trying to bottle the frustration and the rage, but it only bubbled over more and more.

"Fight it!" That sounded vaguely like Soren. "C'mon, Mik, fight it! Don't fight Tai, fight this!"

Finally, a slap of pain across his face. Mikael stared at Soren, shocked at the audacity. "You—" And then he could feel the blood draining from his body, the adrenaline wearing off as he began to shake. "Ancestors—"

Soren nodded. "You're welcome." He nudged Mikael toward Katjin, who was also shaking quietly. "This is why you need to follow whatever Tai says, annoying as it is." Soren's brown eyes were huge, his face pale. "We can't have you cracking up like that all the time, not when it's just gonna get worse."

Mikael inhaled, then breathed out again. "Okay." He tried to focus on the meditation, tried to breathe in the good and let out the bad. He could feel Katjin's breathing echo in time with his. "Okay."

Tai stood a few lengths away, a patrol group clustered behind him. The four Shahi stared at Mikael as if he was a nari cat or something. Mik didn't know if he should wave, or just ignore them. As if anything would reassure them.

"Soren might have a point," Katjin muttered, resting his chin on Mikael's shoulder. "Especially if we keep losing control."

Mikael snorted. "Control?"

Katjin waved toward Tai. "That's what he's here to teach us." He shrugged. "Maybe we should let him. For a little while."

And so it went. They trained, though not without the occasional gripe at what seemed like a series of useless exercises. While the Shahi kept their distance, 'Shahi demon' started to seem like an epithet now. Mikael was starting to think of Tai and Aidan as just being people. Sure, Tai could manipulate energy into whatever he wanted and Aidan's gift was supposed to be even stronger, but that didn't mean that they'd necessarily use it to roast Lowland babies or anything. He still had more misgivings about the father than the son, though. Tai's motives for helping them, whatever they were, didn't exactly seem pure. Aidan, on the other hand, just seemed outright curious, even if it annoyed Katjin at how much he hung around.

"He follows you with his eyes! It's... creepy," Katjin said as they circled around each other with their staves, a careful arm's length apart. "Like he's a puppy or something, waiting for affection."

"Maybe he likes Mikael," Soren said. "Mik, guard higher. Katjin has easy access to your ribs." As if to prove his point, he poked Mikael in the ribs with his own staff as he circled outside the two of them. "Mik's handsome, especially now that he's filled out. He's exotic, since no one here really has blond hair."

"No one has dark hair either," Mikael pointed out, following Katjin's careful actions with his eyes, trying to read the clues Kat's body gave off about what he would do next. "You're more exotic. And better looking." He flashed a quick grin at Soren. "Well, maybe not you, but Katjin is."

The Shahi still seemed strange to him, their faces too triangular, their pointed ears too foreign. The broad, wide-cheeked faces of the Clanfolk and Highlandfolk seemed so much more expressive, so much more comforting. He wouldn't deny the pleasurable twist in his stomach whenever he thought about Katjin, either, and that wasn't just because Katjin had saved him.

He stopped, staring at Katjin. Neither of them talked about it, how much of their attraction to each other was the bond and how much of it was how they felt about each other. He'd hated Katjin at first, almost as much as he hated Soren, but after he was kidnapped, those feelings had suddenly shifted. Well, maybe they hadn't shifted that quickly, but he'd finally figured out what he was trying to deny. While he kept pushing away Katjin's touch, especially after not having been touched in, well… it was still something he wanted more than anything. And he hated his body for that, hated that need.

Something poked him in the gut, knocking the wind out of him. "Pay attention!" Soren said, poking him again, a little softer this time. "If you don't pay attention, how can this help you?"

"How can this help us at all?" Katjin asked, throwing down his staff. Then he picked it up and leaned it against the hirh, looking repentant. He came over, automatically linking his fingers with Mikael. "We're not really any better off with the whole distance thing."

"They didn't build the City in a day," Soren reminded them. "Everything takes time."

But Mikael could feel Katjin's impatience, his urgent need to go and fix things. Mik knew that every day that passed, chances grew slimmer and slimmer of them finding their relatives. He himself had pretty much given up hope that Mother and Father and his sisters were still alive, if they were in the hands of the Empire. No one returned from Empire custody.

"We can't stay here forever," Katjin said in a low voice. "We have to go back sometime." His fingers tightened on Mikael's.

Soren threw an arm around Katjin's neck, rubbing his knuckles against Katjin's flyaway dark hair. "I know, Little Kat." Katjin scowled at the nickname. "That's why we do what we can every day to speed this whole thing up."

The annoying exercises: finding people by emotion, separating out the individual emotions in the hirhai, separating the emotions that only belonged to one person—they all seemed so futile sometimes. As did the excessive meditation. Half the time, Mikael wondered if Katjin was just asleep at his back. The stick-fighting, the sparring, the dancing and the ladders that Tai made them climb endlessly at least seemed to be working toward a goal, lessening the hold of the bond on them. Maybe if he thought about it that way…

"To speed it up," Mikael repeated. "Small steps, aye?" He stepped a stride or two away from Katjin, until he was at their limit of five strides away. He held on as long as he could before the pain got to be too much, shooting warning fits up the bond to let him know that he was pushing it.

"Small steps," Katjin repeated. "I guess we really can't take down an entire empire at once."

Chapter Four

It rained at least every other day, until even Katjin and Soren appreciated the waterproofing capabilities of wood. While Clan yer seemed to do a decent job of keeping off rain, there were still occasions in winter where yer leaked, getting everything and everyone inside wet. They bathed in buckets, washing a limb at a time until they were all longing to jump in a river or pond somewhere. They tried to wash their robes in the same buckets, but that never quite seemed to work. While Mikael and even Soren seemed to eye the Shahi leathers, especially after the tenth time in a day Mik caught his robe on some wayward branch or another, Katjin clung stubbornly to Clan dress. Soren was actually chattering a few phrases in Shahi by the end of their seventh day. He, at least, actually interacted with more people than just Tai and Aidan. Katjin still eyed the trees around them with the same suspicion that he gave Aidan, but at least there weren't any more panic attacks. Well, not until they finally saw a moah and a nari.

They finally figured out exactly why rhythm was such a taboo topic in the hirhai. Soren had only laughed at the outcome, and said it was "just like Kat" to pull something like that off.

It started off simply enough. Soren was off scouting, Aidan was actually nowhere to be found and Tai was 'busy' with something. As much fun as it was to stare up at the roof of the hirh and wonder how long it would take for rain to drip through the thatch, Mikael was feeling antsy. He'd all but threatened to tie Katjin's hands together if his bonded didn't stop fidgeting. First, Katjin had picked up the bowls from breakfast, picking at the dried porridge residue left on the stoneware. Then, Kat walked over to the ladder and moved it back and forth until he'd found a place for it that better suited him—right back where it had started. Luckily, the hirh was so small that Katjin could pace and fidget and wander to his heart's content, without bothering the bond too much. At this point, the pain was more of an annoyance anyway—and nothing was more annoying than watching Katjin idly fidget.

"Let's go," Mikael finally said, standing up and hauling Katjin out the hirh door.

"It's raining!" Katjin whined, trying to shake Mikael's hand off. "We'll get wet." Someone was getting spoiled by regularly having a non-leaking roof over his head.

"And you'll melt away. C'mon."

Instead of heading into the center of the hirhai, Mikael herded Katjin south, out toward the forest. There were still plenty of walkways here, though they tended to be railed only on one side, rather than the double-sided railings that protected the walkways weaving in and out of the hirh. They still proceeded carefully, though. Tai had provided them with sturdy leather boots, soles studded with small metal pegs to help them keep their grip on the slippery branches, but even those weren't a safeguard at falling out of a tree. They knew by now that babies were spelled within an inch of their lives, especially when they were just learning how to toddle around. Mikael wondered how many generations of Shahi had been lost before that trick was discovered.

They made their way through the trees, Katjin complaining every now and then as a drip slipped down the neck of his robe. Mikael's peaked cap kept off most of the rain, but the tree branches grabbed at his robes when he pressed too close, almost as if the trees themselves were trying to fend him off.

"You hear that?" Katjin asked suddenly, freezing in place.

Mikael listened, but still heard nothing. "Maybe it's rain in your ears. Or bugs." He smirked at Kat.

"Just because those grasshoppers were in my ears—" Katjin started, before smirking back. "You're not allowed to hang out with Soren anymore."

"And who's going to stop me?" Mikael asked, his grin widening. "You?"

Then he heard it. tap-TAP. tap-tap-TAP.

Katjin shot him a know-it-all look. *See?*

The tapping echoed through out the silent forest, cutting through the stillness like thunder. Arching his eyebrows at Katjin, Mikael nodded in the direction that he thought the sound was coming from. Katjin nodded back.

They moved out quickly, trying to stealth along as quietly as they could. They didn't go far before they came across a Shahi, two trees distant and several branches below. She knelt on a small platform in the crotch of a tree, drum in hand as she beat out the rhythm again.

tap-TAP.

With a soft snicker, Katjin beat out the response. tap-

TAP-TAP.

The Shahi's red head came up, funny yellow eyes scanning the trees for something. Her eyes passed right over the tree where Katjin and Mikael hid, much to Mik's surprise. Then, bending her head over her drum again, she tapped.

tap-TAP-TAP.

The rhythm was almost compelling, especially after so many days of not hearing any. This time, it was Mikael who responded: tap-TAP TAP-tap-TAP.

They beat back and forth, until Mikael noticed that it was growing awfully warm, where they sat. Sweat poured down the Shahi woman's face, and he could feel her growing more frantic. Her eyes stared off into the distance, looking almost lost.

"Mik—" Katjin hissed. "I think—"

And then the world exploded, raining sticky red jelly down onto their heads.

"Shite!" Katjin whispered. "Run, Mik. Run!"

They ran back toward the hirhai, wanting to get away from the scene of the crime as fast as they could. They had just made it back to their hirh when they saw Soren standing in the doorway, stopping them dead in their tracks.

"I don't even want to know," he said, "but if Tai catches you, he'll probably get out that stick of his again and use it for demonic purposes."

Katjin went pale. "Buckets," Mikael said quickly. "We need buckets."

That's how they learned about the difficulties of trying to bathe thoroughly in a bucket, and how hard it was to get your robe clean at the same time.

That night, Tai brought them dinner. He sniffed,

but shook his head. "You lads been at the redfruit?" he asked as he set the platter down on the table. "Ariana mentioned an unseasonable bloom of it today, apparently bursting all over the southern walkways. Took her scouts half the afternoon to clean up." He shrugged. "Maybe some stronger soap…"

After half a moon, Tai finally decided to take them down to the forest floor. Apparently some Shahi went their entire lives without setting foot down there, using the 'high roads' to get from hirhai to hirhai. It was a little more difficult now, since the Shahi population had dwindled since the plague over three hundred years before, but it could still be done.

"Time was that there were hirhai a two-day's walk from each other, and halfway hirh in between," Tai said one night. "Now, with as much forest as we could want and game besides, there are fewer and fewer born each generation."

Their hirhai was called Corralei, and apparently it had some sort of history to it, because the only Shahi King and Queen of the City had been born here. Mikael still wasn't exactly sure who this Rhyssalia and Tormathron were, but apparently they'd united the Cityfolk and the Shahi much as the Empire had done with the Lowlanders, Clanfolk and Highlandfolk. The Black and the Gold, however, were a little more successful. Their peace, though, had been fleeting, and in their granddaughter's reign, the plague struck, decimating the population of the Cityfolk and taking nearly a quarter of the Shahi with them.

"There was thought, for a while, that the plague was something the Empire cooked up," Tai had said. "If that had been in their capabilities, doubtlessly they would have used it again. Now, though, we know it was just a matter of fate. Blood-line curses we've had plenty, but when it comes to nature, it's hard to overcome."

They'd reached a sufficient point in their training that Mikael and Katjin actually made it down to one of the lowest platforms without falling off the ladders. Tai didn't want to tempt fate too much and actually take them all the way down to the forest floor. They went backward, feet first. Mikael could hear Katjin above him singing softly the whole time. Smiling slightly as he made his way down, Mikael sung back to him. First, it was the aiding song. Then Katjin launched into drinking song after bawdy drinking song, ones that Mikael had only heard at the seasonal feast days, when the servants at the country house drank far into the night. As much as Mikael liked to think of himself as a man of the world, Katjin had obviously seen and experienced so much more. That was what happened, though, when you were locked into a room your whole life. He'd had the solitude of the country and the occasional visit to Stoneridge, but he'd seen nowhere near what Katjin had.

The platform they finally came to was only a few strides above the ground, what Tai proclaimed as 'just out of moah reach'.

"But moah aren't meat eaters, right?" Mikael asked for the hundredth time. "Just leaves?"

Tai rolled his eyes, but nodded before waving Mik quiet. Their Shahi teacher didn't seem to be the most patient man, and Mikael often wondered exactly how much experience he had with people from over the mountain.

"Sorry," Mikael said, a little wounded. It was an honest question. It wasn't as if there was a dearth of information available on the Shahi. Starless hells, they'd only just admitted that the Shahi might not be demons who drank blood.

Aidan poked at Mikael, giving him a slight smile. That helped, at least. While Tai didn't seem especially happy about Aidan trying to spend time with them, he begrudgingly allowed it. Mikael was still curious about this blood bond Aidan supposedly had, but their language barriers were still firmly in place, even after half a moon of constant company.

Tai motioned for them to come forward to the edge of the platform and lie on their stomachs. Mikael and Katjin complied, though the sudden appearance of the ground about four strides below was a little disconcerting. Mikael had to breathe deeply a few times to calm himself. At least none of them had puked over the side of the platform. Soren said it was probably only a matter of time, since winter winds howled through the hirhai something furious, rocking the entire treetops.

Something else to look forward to.

Laying on his belly, Mikael stared out at the endless green, wondering exactly what—or who—they were waiting for. The forest floor seemed choked with endless underbrush and decaying fallen trunks, everything hung with moss of every shade of green. It was almost blinding. Even the undergrowth seemed higher than Mikael's head, as if the forest itself were on a giant scale.

There was a rustling in the undergrowth just below their heads. Mikael's heart stopped and he held his breath. A small russet head poked out of the bushes, and a ground hen clucked its way into the clearing, pecking at the grass. Beside him, Katjin shook slightly with silent laughter. Mikael elbowed him none-too-gently, grinning in return.

As the ground hen, looking almost exactly like the chickens he'd chased so often at home, pecked at the ground, he could hear a second rustling in the bushes. The hen itself seemed unconcerned, foraging as if there was nothing wrong in the world, but Mikael couldn't help but feel a sense of dread.

And then a flash of black and rumbling growl.

All that was left of the ground hen were some red feathers, and a huge black cat sat in the middle of the clearing, looking quite satisfied with itself.

Mikael shoved a fist in his mouth, trying not to make a noise. The cat was huge—almost the size of a small pony. Maybe that's why those moah birds were as large as the Shahi said. They'd have to be, to put up any kind of a fight against that.

"Nari," came Aidan's soft whisper. Luckily, the nari cat was too busy washing its paws to apparently notice.

Snack was more like it. He couldn't imagine such a large, lean beast going after a mere chicken for a meal. Suddenly, he wondered how high those cats could jump.

Before Mikael knew it, his feet were on the ladder, propelling him upward into the canopy. From the panting behind him, he knew Katjin was right at his heels. They didn't stop climbing until they reached the next platform, another ten strides up. As soon as Katjin made it up onto the platform, Mikael grabbed him, clinging tight. "Shite," Mikael muttered, face pressed against Katjin's sweaty neck. "Now I know why they stay in trees."

"Ancestors bless," Katjin said. "All that, just for a

little chicken." He shuddered. "I can only imagine what it would do to us."

"And that's *not* what's howling at night?" Mikael asked, pulling back a little. He could hear feet on the ladder rungs, hurrying their way up.

"No, the howling you hear is the moah," Tai said as his head appeared at the end of the platform. Even he looked a little pale. "Nari don't usually get that close."

"That's why you have scouts then," Katjin said, somewhat calmer now. Mikael could no longer feel Katjin's pulse jumping in his neck.

Tai nodded. "When they Cityfolk left, they abandoned a lot of their herds. Some of them wandered into the forest, so a feral cow or sheep will occasionally stray this close to the mountains. The nari sometimes hunt those, when they aren't trying to take down moah."

"And the moah are the height of men?" Katjin asked, voice shaking a bit. "They're the ones that scream like that."

Again, the nod from Tai. "You usually won't hear a nari coming. Most of them don't bother to climb this high, so you should be safe."

Mikael gulped. "Most?"

Tai looked surprised. "Why do you think we built our hirhai so high?"

He didn't want to admit that he'd wondered that very thing, and had hoped the altitude of the hirhai was more of an aesthetic purpose than one of personal safety.

"Ancestors bless for that," Katjin muttered, "though they would probably exile me from the Clans for saying that."

Tai left them to their own devices that afternoon. Aidan, however, seemed anxious to hang around. Given that it was a free platform that didn't belong to them, Mikael didn't see how they could actually get rid of Aidan, especially since he lived in the hirhai and they were just guests.

Katjin held the hem of his robe between two hands as Mikael reinforced the stitching one more time. "I think you're getting taller," he said around the needle in his mouth. "We might have to let this one down soon."

His bonded's face brightened at that. "Really?" It was a second-hand robe—all of theirs were—but even Mikael could see how it was hanging shorter on Katjin's legs, not quite hitting his calves anymore.

"Might have to leave off our robes altogether," Soren said, poking his fingers through a hole in his sleeve. "Mine keeps catching on branches when we scout. The others have started making fun of me."

Katjin scowled at his cousin. "We can't give up our robes. What would we wear, leather?" Leather, as far as Clanfolk seemed concerned, was suitable only for boots and tack. Maybe armor, if the lacquered Clan armor wasn't available, but never clothing. They were too proud of their weaving for that.

This once, Mikael didn't feel like stepping in as peacekeeper. It was usually Katjin's job, since he and Soren were the ones most often going at it. Katjin did a really good job of ignoring his cousin's jibes, which had lost their viciousness over the summer. Before he could say anything, though, Soren stood up. "My turn for patrol. Don't get into too much trouble."

As soon as he left, Aidan seemed to see that as his opportunity.

"See moah?" he said. "We go down." He pointed.

Mikael exchanged a look with Katjin, who looked suspiciously at Aidan. "Where's your apa?" Katjin asked in an almost accusing tone.

"Tai?" Aidan sounded surprised. "Gone." He waved his hands in the vague direction of the hirhai center. "Go down?"

He hated to admit that curiosity was getting the better of him. "It's a chance to see the ground," he pointed out to Kat. He didn't quite whine, but even he could hear the longing in his voice.

Katjin smiled slightly. "Ground. Steady, under our feet, without air between us and it."

"And just imagine how jealous Soren would be," Mikael continued, smirking slightly. From what he knew, the scouts tended to stay in the security of the trees when they patrolled. They didn't just look out for nari or moah in the area, but also make sure that pathways were unbroken and safe for people to use.

They went down the same way they'd come up. This time, going down the ladder seemed a little easier, even though Mikael kept listening for the telltale rustle in the bushes that meant a nari cat might be nearby. As the silence built on their way down, though, his fears soon slipped into the back of his mind.

When his feet hit the ground, it was all Mikael could do not to fall to his knees and kiss the solid earth. Katjin's green eyes were almost feverish and his bonded did actually hit the ground on his knees, but Mikael thought that was due more to dizziness than giving thanks for the ground beneath his feet.

"We made it," Mikael said softly, hooking an arm around Katjin's neck. "See, it wasn't so bad."

Katjin gave him a shaky grin, his legs quivering slightly as if from the very effort of the climb down. "Ancestors, then we have to go back up!"

Mikael snorted. "What goes down, Kat…"

His bonded made a face.

Aidan hissed at them, waving for them to be quiet. Mikael tensed, a sudden rush of adrenaline shooting through his body. Katjin's quivering seemed to turn from fear into excitement, and he was all but vibrating again.

"If those big birds can sense movement in the earth likes snakes can, you'll bring the whole herd down on us," Mikael muttered. "Stop it." Katjin's bouncing was beginning to make him uneasy. Aidan didn't need two of them wound tighter than a bow string, especially if it would attract the attention of that giant cat again.

Aidan's head was up, his nostrils flaring. Mikael wondered if he was scenting the air or trying to pick up some clue that was obviously invisible to him and Katjin. Katjin, for all his anxiousness, froze. His bonded would have some sense of survival, when it came to the wild. Kat and his Apa did spend most of their time crossing the plains, which, while hospitable, weren't without their dangers. Although, at least on the plains, you didn't have to worry about giant birds and cats mowing you down.

Something thrashed in the underbrush ahead of them. Like the forest they'd crept through to escape the cavalry on the other side of the mountain, the trees here were draped in moss. Unlike that forest, though, the underbrush was thick, hampering sight lines and crowding whatever trail they were on. Rocks were strewn here and there—not small ones, but almost house-sized boulders. These, too, wore a heavy layer of greenery. From the amount of rain they'd had in the past half a moon, Mikael could only imagine how much water actually fell to keep the ground so spongy and the moss so green. In fact, he was beginning to feel a bit of the humidity that you didn't quite seem to feel at hirh-height. He squirmed in his heavy robe, wondering if he'd be insulting the Horse Clanfolk if he left it behind somewhere.

They moved deeper into the underbrush. Mikael alternated between watching Aidan's leather-clad back for direction and focusing on his feet, so that he wouldn't trip over a wayward root or rock. He stumbled a couple times, nearly pulling Katjin down on top of him. Luckily, Aidan always seemed to be there to right the two of them.

Water dripped down his neck occasionally. He could hear Katjin cursing quietly behind him. Aidan would look back every now and then, as if unimpressed with their ability to stealth through the undergrowth. What was Aidan honestly expecting? Katjin had never been near trees, and Mikael wasn't exactly forester material. The Empire had long since deemed the woods near Stoneridge to be free of bandits and other dangers. No cavalry or foresters had patrolled those woods for years. The forests of his childhood had been nothing compared to this. Down here, the dappled light seemed closer to twilight, even though Mikael knew that it was closer to noon meal.

Aidan stopped so suddenly that Mikael bumped into him. Before Mik could apologize, Aidan put one finger to his lips to signal for quiet. Mik nodded, passing the sign back to Katjin. Before anyone could say anything, though, they heard the scream.

It was the same weird howling that they'd heard that first night, chilling Mikael to the very marrow in his bones. Beside him, Katjin shivered. Mikael hummed as quietly as he could, hoping that even the vibrations of his throat would soothe Kat a little bit. Katjin squeezed his hand, giving him a slight smile. The gesture was obviously appreciated.

At least they knew it wasn't a nari cat. The rustling in the bushes was too high up. It looked like it was even higher up than his head.

Aidan grabbed at them both, dragging them into the underbrush. His eyes were fierce, his commandment understood: stay, don't move, don't say a word.

Katjin's hand fumbled for his knife, still thrust deep in his sash as it had been for the past four moons. Mikael knew he should have been carrying some kind of weapon, especially after what happened in the cavalry camp, but it had never been a habit with him. While his father had started him in staff training when he was still small, carrying anything larger than an eating dagger had never been a habit with him. He'd never been at risk, not in the protected life he'd led.

Before Mikael could grab on to a weapon he didn't have, though, the creature stepped out of the underbrush. Its head appeared first, a broad-beaked face not unlike a duck's or other water fowl. The head was freakishly high, though, standing somewhere around four strides tall, if Mikael's eye was any measure. The head was followed by the impossibly long, feathered neck, culminating in a thick, muscular body and huge, sturdy legs. The shoulder of the bird alone was probably higher than his head.

"Doesn't look like a chicken," Katjin whispered.

At least it didn't look too dangerous, if you discounted the size and the talons on its plate-sized feet that looked longer than his or Katjin's hands.

"Stars," Mikael whispered. "It's..." Its feathers were a glossy mottled brown and green, allowing it to fade in easily with the underbrush. It seemed nearly twice his height, towering over the very tallest of the underbrush. It dropped its long neck, using the length to probe deep into the underbrush for whatever it ate. Mikael noticed that some of the branches in the undergrowth were completely stripped of leaves. That reassured him a little bit, that the beast didn't eat meat. He could only imagine how powerful those jaws were.

The bird extracted its head from the underbrush, this time chewing a mouthful of leaves. Its fist-sized dark eyes whirled, as if taking in the scenery around it. It ruffled its wings, but from where he was, Mikael could see that they were just vestigial wings. The moah probably couldn't fly, or if it could, it wouldn't get too far. The long talons on the feet suddenly made sense. It would be easy to slash a nari cat with those talons, which themselves looked longer than his hand.

A branch snapped somewhere behind them. The moah's head came up, and it froze for a moment, as if poised for flight. Then the underbrush exploded with a fury of black fur.

"No!" Aidan screamed.

And just as suddenly, the bush surrounding the moah burst into flame.

The nari cat snarled, batting at the flames before running off into the bushes in the other direction. The moah itself ran *through* the flames and out the other side, trailing bits of fiery branches behind it. They could still hear it, trampling its way through the underbrush.

Before the fire could spread, Mikael ran toward it. He took off his robe and began to beat at the fire. It wasn't a large fire. The moisture in the underbrush seemed to keep it from burning too far or too fast.

Katjin was at his side, doing the same with his robe. It didn't take long to put it out. When they turned around to look at Aidan, all they could do was stare.

The Shahi, though, looked nonchalant about it.

"Up," Aidan said, pointing to a tree with shallow handholds carved out of its trunk "Back up now."

Shrugging back into their charred robes, Mikael and Katjin dutifully followed him up, which was a lot harder than down. Though his feet seemed to find the footholds pretty easily, the hem of his robe kept getting caught under his feet. It gave him a few heart-stopping moments as he fought to find his footing again.

When they reached the first crotch of their tree, Mikael took off his robe, bundling it up. "I can't take it!" he shouted, ready to hurl the damned thing down to the forest floor below. "Stupid *trees*. Just admit it, Kat. You can't wear a damned robe in the trees." Before he could throw the wadded up bundle, though, Aidan took it from him.

Aidan quickly unrolled and rerolled it, securing it with some leather cording he pulled out of his belt pouch. "Here," Aidan said, an almost kind look on his face. "Wear over." He settled the cording like a strap over Mikael's shoulder, then held out another loop of leather to Katjin. "Not hurt. Roll."

Katjin's green eyes wavered, then, to Mikael's surprise, his bonded actually shrugged out of his robe and carefully rolled it up. He tied it with the same care Aidan had shown, stowing it over one shoulder just as Mik's was.

"Just this once," Katjin said in a low voice.

Aidan nodded, tapping Katjin's shoulder with two

careful fingers. "Good Kat." Then, to Mik's surprise, Aidan actually grinned. "Good Kat. Bad nari cat."

Katjin sighed with long-suffering patience. "Go talk to Soren about that."

They made it back up to the main platforms of the hirhai without much more fuss. As soon as they hit the top of the ladder, Katjin unrolled his robe and immediately slid into it. His face visibly relaxed as soon as he was wrapped in the worn robe.

Then, Mikael was faced with an expectant Katjin. Aidan, too, seemed caught up in the moment, watching Mikael to see what he'd do.

Mik sighed. "It's too damned hot, the robe's wearing out anyway, and I might as well save it for winter when it's cold." That was assuming they would be here for winter, since he had a feeling that the pass became inhospitable as soon as the first snows hit. Coming across in summer had been bad enough. He couldn't even imagine clinging to those narrow trails hip-deep in snow—not that he'd ever seen that much snow in his life.

Katjin looked disappointed, but Mikael couldn't help it. Resisting the urge to roll his eyes, he slipped an arm around Katjin's shoulders. "Besides, while I can fix robes, I don't think I could sew you an entire new one. Let me save mine for when we go home, so we can go back in style." That return trip over the mountains still seemed like more of an 'if' to him, but he wasn't going to tell Katjin that.

Not yet.

"I think I've figured it out," Soren said that night, as they ate dinner. Soren, of course, had heard some garbled version of the day's adventures from Aidan in whatever passed for their secret Shahi language.

"Figured what out?" Katjin asked around a mouthful of stew. As usual, Tai had left them with wooden bowls of stew and a loaf of the bread that was made from nut flour. It wasn't as crusty as Mikael was used to and had an odd aftertaste, but it was great to sop up leftover stew.

"Figured out why the Shahi all look at you funny. And why Tai's afraid of his own son."

Mikael almost dropped his bowl of stew. "What?" He stared at Soren, who looked serious.

"Think about it," Soren said, leaning back against the hirh wall as he sat on the bench across the table from them. "Aidan said that he was bound at some point. What if their binding does what it did to you two? What if it doubles their power or something?"

Mikael could feel Katjin's shudder. "After what Aidan did to the nari this afternoon—" He shook his head. "Tai did mention how they broke up the song-lines, so that no one person would hold all the magic."

Soren nodded. "Exactly. So here's this society where they've banned any rhythms that can create out-of-control power surges, and here you two come, explosive and uncontrolled—"

"We're working on it," Mikael cut in.

With a negligent wave of his hand, Soren brushed Mikael off. "Anyway. Here you two come, like firebrands, and the Shahi don't know how to cope. I think that's why they avoid us."

"Us?" Mikael arched an eyebrow.

"Us," Soren repeated. "They might let me patrol with

them, but it isn't like they're busting down the door, trying to be my friend. None of them, boys or girls alike."

"Is that what this is about? Your lack of creature comfort?" Katjin asked, rolling his eyes.

Soren sighed. "It's not just that. It's—" He shook his head. "Never mind. Never mind how others see you. Never mind."

"But—" Mikael tried to protest, but Soren had obviously fallen into a mood and would refuse to be beguiled out of it.

"Never mind," Soren repeated, and that was the end of that.

Chapter Five

"No, try again. Remember: in unison," Tai said. Half a moon later. In the days following the incident with the moah, Aidan had appeared to be avoiding them. Mikael wasn't sure if this was actually Aidan's own idea, or if Tai had somehow clued into Katjin's obvious dislike of Aidan and forcibly kept his son away. Instead of illicit trips down to the forest floor, their days were spent doing exercises and practicing, til Mikael actually looked back to their camp in the valley with longing for something less boring.

This time, instead of facing each other, Katjin and Mikael stood next to each other as they both attempted the defensive pass of staff-work. Shadowdancing was too much for them to attempt together; their difference in their abilities with edged weapons was too great. Soren said that only really gifted fighters actually accomplished shadowdancing. It was something to be proud of accomplishing, but something that was rare even among the Shahi.

Staff resting on the ground, Mikael gripped the staff with both hands, about half an arm's length apart. Tai beat a drum in time to their movements in that odd off-beat and complicated style that the Shahi preferred.

Beat. "Shoulder." Mikael raised his top hand to shoulder height, bringing the staff with it.

Beat. "Head." Now, up to head height. Out of the corner of his eye, he could see Katjin doing the same.

Beat. "Thrust." They dropped their staves back to shoulder height again, pushing the staves out with their arms, still perpendicular to the ground.

Straight moves over, now, is where it got complicated.

Beat. "Pivot." As one, they both pivoted on their rear foot, turning left. Beat. "X." Tipping his top hand forward and bringing the bottom of the staff up, Mikael slashed an X in the air, careful not to hit Katjin on the head.

Beat. "Cross." A twist of his hip and a step forward, and Mikael cut a cross with the tip of his staff.

Beat. "Circle parry." As Mikael whipped his staff through the air into the clover-leaf pattern that formed the full circle parry, the tip of his staff caught on Katjin's. Mikael arched his staff back, sliding into position to face Katjin. Kat grinned at him.

"No. No!" Tai cut in, pushing them apart before they could attempt to brain each other with their staves. "Unison. What had I said about unison?" He sighed. "Put the staves away. It's back to breathing again."

This time, it was Katjin's turn to sigh. Mikael could feel the tension in Katjin's body, the impatience. Mikael breathed in deep, trying to calm his own nerves in an attempt to quell Katjin's fidgets. "Easy," he said softly, touching Katjin's fingers with his own. "You know we have to take it a step at a time."

"So we can be a staff-dancing team?" Katjin asked sourly. "We'll stun the cavalry with our ability to keep them at bay, one staff stroke at a time." Katjin's hand found his, a sense of relief flooding through Mikael's body at the touch.

"But we're doing it," Mikael reminded him, trying to channel some of the forced calm he felt. "We were apart for a good while."

Katjin nodded begrudgingly. "There is that."

Tai had them sit back to back, so that they could feel the other inhale and exhale. Tai had them breathing in the same sort of rhythms that they were using in staff-work: one inhaled, while the other exhaled. There was also pattern work, which usually made Mikael out of breath and cross.

"In, two, three, four." Each count was punctuated by a drum beat. There were times when Mikael wanted to beat Tai over the head with the drum.

"Out, two, three, four." For now, they just breathed in and out as they were told, blanking their mind. Mikael hated to admit it, but the relaxation did do him some good. Even if he wasn't sure about this whole channeling thing, since he knew that neither of them had any talent when it came to magical energies, much less good and bad energies, it still took some of the tension out of the two of them.

They breathed in and out for a few minutes more, until Tai told them to stop.

They opened their eyes to find Tai staring at them. Uneasy, Mikael wound his fingers through Katjin's again, more out of comfort than anything else.

"You're off somehow," Tai said, almost to himself. "You're almost completely in-line with everything, except you're off by just one beat." He pointed at Katjin. "You're tone-deaf. I think it's you."

"Now—" Mikael broke in, jumping to Katjin's protection. "You have no right."

Tai looked at him with those strange yellow-gold eyes. "I have every right," the Shahi said. "I'm your teacher. And if you won't submit to my techniques, then I won't teach you."

Mikael was beginning to wonder why Mandric left them in the hands of this nut.

"I can't separate the two of you until you learn to live in complete harmony," Tai went on. "Our own bonded have none of the issues that you do."

"Your own—" Mikael stared. Maybe all that nonsense Soren had spewed all those nights ago was actually true, somehow. "You bind people like this? Deliberately?"

"Weren't you paying attention?" Tai asked, exasperated. "Where do you think these exercises come from, that I'm making them up as we go?"

Unless they bound people together for magic principles, though Mikael couldn't quite see how that would help. Aidan said he was bound. If they didn't bind to augment power, then maybe Aidan was a lock on someone's ability? Or the key to it?

"Time for drastic measures," Tai said. Before either of them could react, he pried them apart, standing between them. "This is your next test: no touching til the end of the day."

Mikael's jaw dropped. "You can't do that!" he said, automatically reaching for Katjin. Before their hands could touch, Tai brought one of the staves down, stinging Mikael's hand.

"No touching," he repeated. "If you can't learn to work completely together, we'll separate you the hard way."

The Shahi had been reluctant to get anywhere near Mikael so far. Even Soren and Aidan kept their distance—Aidan especially, after Mikael's reaction to that one quick embrace—neither of them touching, since physical contact made the 'pathy all the stronger. Katjin's physical touch had provided some relief to that, though. After so long without touching, and then the sudden constant need to be in Katjin's presence, he couldn't survive without that touch.

Scowling, he breathed deeply, noticing Katjin doing the same thing. Mikael gripped his hands together, trying to keep from reaching out to Katjin. Katjin seemed to be doing the same thing, since he was fidgeting with his sash.

They stared at each other, Tai slipping his staff pointedly between them everytime they gravitated toward each other. Something bothered Mikael about Tai's attitude toward the whole thing, wondering if this was some sort of exercise to show Tai's dominance over them or something. Not that Tai was a bad guy, he just kind of confused Mikael every now and then.

"Da?" Aidan's voice called. "Mandric comes!"

Just as Mikael was reaching for Katjin, Tai hit him with the staff again. "No touching!" he barked, sounding almost as bad as Soren. He looked at the two of them. "Might as well go see what Mandric has to say."

Mandric had left in such a rush that it was all Mikael could do not to rush into the Highlandfolk's arms the minute he saw Mandric. Tai kept at his heels, all the time threatening with that bedamned staff every time Mikael got near Kat. One of these days, he was going to do nasty things to Tai with that stick.

"Mandric!" Katjin launched himself at Mandric, only

to be followed by Mikael. Mik held back, waiting until Kat was done before hugging Mandric hard. "Have you found them?"

Katjin's face was lit up with anticipation, his heart beating so fast that Mikael could feel it, even though they weren't touching.

"You aren't—" Mandric began, staring at them with wonder. "You aren't touching."

Mikael scowled at Tai. "He won't let us," he muttered in Lowlander. "Keeps thwapping us with that stupid stick every time we try."

Mandric looked thoughtful. "I hadn't thought about that. If what you two have is some kind of a dependency on each other…" He said something to Tai in Shahi that Mikael didn't quite catch, nodding at the answer he received. "In answer to your question, Kat, aye, I did find them."

The Highlandfolk tried his hardest to hide it, but Mikael could still pick up on the sorrow that laced through the excitement. At Katjin's fallen face, that meant that his bonded could, too, even without touching.

"Meke and Febe?" Katjin asked, voice actually shaking.

"Your meke and febe are alive," Mandric said slowly, now not looking at Soren, who had arrived from somewhere. "The rest of the adults, though…"

A quick look at Soren showed him physically shaking, hands clenched so tight that his knuckles were white, his forehead wrinkling with effort at keeping his eyes closed. Katjin put a hand on his cousin's arm, whispering something to Soren. Even Katjin seemed tensed, trying to control his own emotional overload. After a few moments, Soren's body relaxed a little bit, though his eyes still remained stubbornly closed. Mikael didn't blame him.

Mikael swallowed hard, trying to calm his breathing. "So they took the oldest and youngest and—" He couldn't continue. As Katjin's breathing began to increase into a panic, Mikael fought his control. He breathed in and out, in time with the slow beat of the aiding song. He could hear Katjin humming it, the tune sounded ragged around Katjin's labored breathing.

"Apa and Ama?" Soren asked, his face pale, as if he wasn't sure he wanted the confirmation. He, at least, seemed a little calmer, leaving Mikael to try and comfort Katjin.

Mandric shook his head. "Anyone over sixteen, lad," he said gruffly, "including your aunties and uncles."

Starless— "Hells!" Mikael screamed, turning around and punching the closest tree trunk. He beat at the bark, well-aware of the tears that burned their course down his face. He beat and beat, just as he used to beat at the walls of that stone room. His knuckles were on fire, and he could smell the blood. Half of him had been content to stay here, where the Empire had no reach. But that was cowardice, and the Empire...

A hand suddenly blocked his fist's path to the tree. "Easy. Focus, Mik. The rest of the hirhai doesn't need to feel this" Soren's voice said, his strong arms wrapping around Mikael and physically turning him away from the tree.

Mikael gulped, inhaling slowly, deeply. Each time this happened, he was sure that the hirhai would collectively throw them to the nari cats and the moah down below. All they needed was another emotional leak.

"That's it," Soren continued. "You don't need to take it out on something defenseless. Take it out on the Empire.

We might as well use all that energy of yours." His voice was deadly cool and calm.

The burning fear, the helplessness itself was easy enough to channel into anger. He just had to think of the darkness; the slimy, chilling touch of the Empire 'paths mind trying to invade his own. Even the filthy hands of the guards who had held him down, branding Mikael as a 'path with his knife. Mikael rubbed at the faded scar on his wrist. The air started to heat up around him.

"When do we leave?" Mikael asked, unable to look at Katjin. He had to stay strong. He had to channel the rage so that he could use it—and would use it—to make the Empire pay.

"You aren't going anywhere," Tai said suddenly, his face pale. "You're not trained, you're leaking emotions like a sieve, and because of that, they'll see you coming for days." He turned to Mandric, his anger almost coloring the air around him. "Why did you come here now? We were just getting somewhere in their training. You know that it's lost, if they go."

"We have to go," Mikael said, glaring at Tai. This—this demonspawn *Shahi* wasn't going to hold him back any longer. Magic or not, he was nothing, as far as Mikael was concerned. No more fruitless exercises, no more getting hit on the head with that blasted stick. "If we don't go now, if we don't strike now, when they're not expecting—"

"Easy, lad," Mandric said soothingly, putting his hands on Mikael's shoulders. "Let's not rush into anything here."

Mikael slipped out of Mandric's reach, backing up until he was pressed against Katjin's body; Katjin's solidness helped ground the anger, fueling it with the frustration that Mikael needed. "Rush into anything? We've sat here for moons! Waiting for you, waiting for anything! And after all he's done—" Mikael glared at Tai.

And there was new energy, a quicksilver siren-song that burned even brighter than the anger. Mikael could feel it calling to him, calling—

A crackle, and the tree behind Aidan burst into flame. "ENOUGH!"

Mikael shook, gasping for air. Katjin's arms tightened around him, quivering at the same lack of control. If not for Kat's grip, Mikael was sure he'd fall to the floor in a heap.

"That's why they can't leave," Tai hissed. Even Aidan looked stunned, leaning against the platform railing as if he couldn't hold himself up. Water appeared from nowhere, dousing out the fire behind Aidan. "They shouldn't be able to do that. That's why we created the song-lines, to prevent something like them from happening!"

"And you know this is exactly what we need, that this is the chance we've been waiting for," Mandric said in the same quiet tone.

"Firepower," Mikael said, his heart sinking with the realization. If even Mandric only valued them for whatever strange skills they had... "That's all we are. Firepower." He stepped forward, pacing to the limit of his distance from Katjin. He stared at Tai, raising one fist. "You want me and Kat. You won't tell us why, and you won't tell us what you're doing, but you still insist we listen to you."

He could hear humming. It wasn't Katjin humming, though, it was Tai. His normally-pale face was moon-white and sickly looking, like rotten cheese.

Mikael could feel the rage tickling at the edges of his emotions again, the anger that had warmed him and fired up within him just moments before, making his blood sing with power. "You fear us." He took a step forward, knowing Katjin would automatically follow. Knowing Katjin would automatically feed him whatever he needed. Knowing that, somehow, Aidan would as well.

"Mikael," Mandric said softly. "Think. Think about what you're doing. Know your enemy."

He looked at Mandric, noticing how even Mandric faltered slightly when Mikael looked at him.

"If they had access to more of the magic lines," Mandric said, directing his voice toward Tai, "if they consciously worked with your son, they would bring this whole place down, right now."

Tai's voice shook. "Which is why they need to complete their training, here with me."

Mandric only stared down Tai, regret on his face. "And you know they'll follow me the minute I leave," he said. "Which means they'll be lost in the passes, and you'll lose your chance forever, if you haven't lost it already."

"You know the stakes," Tai hissed. "You know what this could cost us."

"And you know what we can and can't do without them," Mandric said finally, resigned. "If they're this fired up now, it's our chance to strike."

Mikael caught Katjin's green eyes, red-rimmed from his own tears. He fought the urge to reach out to his bonded, instead reaching out the most comforting and soothing feelings that he could. He focused the brunt of that on Soren and Katjin, trying to ease their sorrow in the only way he knew, hoping whatever backlash would reach the hirhai as well.

"What chance?" he asked, suspecting that whatever hinged on him was what was making Tai so antsy about training them.

Tai and Mandric exchanged one of those looks. "You're an untrained 'path," Mandric said simply. "While heart-senses aren't rare, the training that the Empire enforces on them usually inhibits them, limiting them. You don't have those limits."

Mikael could only stare at them. "But thought-senses—" He shook his head. "I thought thought-senses were the dangerous ones. So I can figure out what people are feeling. What good does that do?"

"Thought-sensing only works on an individual level," Tai pointed out, looking tired. "You can usually only reach or read one mind at a time. Heart-senses, though, can affect more people. Look at what you did to the cavalry."

"And the camp, after you were rescued," Mandric added, his voice bleak. "While we want you to be able to control that much, so that you don't 'leak' emotions on that scale unless you mean to, you still have nowhere near the limitations that the Empire places on their 'paths."

"So, because Mik doesn't know what he can do, he can do anything?" Katjin asked, his brows furrowed in thought.

"*You* can do anything," Tai said, waving his hand to include Katjin in that. "The two of you together create a force to be reckoned with, and I don't think the Empire realizes that yet." He turned back to Mandric. "Which is why we need them here. To make sure they're ready."

"Except that Nolan says forces are on the move," Mandric countered. "The cavalry has taken no new riders this year, because the Clans refused to send their sons and daughters. Some cavalry have defected, and hide now on the plains. Those who remain don't always follow orders.

Short of declaring actual war, the Empire knows that the Horse Clans are gearing up for something."

"And they refuse to invade," Soren said, wonder in his voice.

Mandric smiled slightly. "They remember the thunder of hooves that the Horse Clan used to make, riding down into the Lowlands with their fire and glory."

"So the others—they fight?" If the Clans were rebelling, maybe something could incite the Lowlanders as well.

Mandric nodded. "Which is why this might be our opportunity, our chance to play you. They don't expect anything like you. The Empire couldn't dream you up in five hundred years."

Mikael blinked, letting it all sink in. "So you've been waiting for us? Waiting for a latent 'path that you can use as part of your great plan?" He wondered if the Shahi had somehow orchestrated all of this, to put him right where they needed to be. "Did you—" He swallowed. "Did you kill my—"

"Mik!" Katjin grabbed him, dragging him close. Before Tai could step in with that damned stick of his, Soren stepped between them and the Shahi.

Katjin shook him slightly. "Mik, you know the risk your apa was taking, hiding you away," he said softly. "I'm surprised they didn't find you earlier, especially if you weren't branded like the rest of us."

Mikael looked at his scarred wrist, the awkwardly carved sigil that marked him as 'path. "Maybe luck was with me, aye?" He rubbed at his wrist. "I just..." He swallowed again around the lump in his throat. "I want it to be an accident. I don't want it to be my fault. I—" It hadn't been real til now, not the way the attack on Katjin's camp had been. It was so much easier to believe that his family was just hiding somewhere, not knowing what their fate was.

If they went back, he'd find out what happened to them. And it would be one more thing he was responsible for.

"Because you asked to be born a 'path,'" Soren said in a fierce tone. "Because you asked for your gift to come late. It's not your fault, Mik. If anything, your apa should've brought you to the Highlands or even here the minute he decided not to have you branded." Soren's arm came around him too, until the three of them huddled together.

Soren looked up at Tai. "We're going, all three of us," he said in a more formal tone. "We appreciate your hospitality and aid and will return it if you ever cross our paths on the plains."

"I go." Aidan moved closer to them, reaching out, but not quite touching Mikael. "I go with. Aye?" His yellow eyes, no longer as strange as they had been, seemed to search Mikael's. "With magic, boom?" His hands mimed an explosion, then he pronounced carefully, "Distraction."

Mikael turned to Tai, suddenly remembering. "Aidan said he was bound. Do you do the blood-rite too?"

Tai barked something at his son in Shahi, who seemed to yell right back in the same vehement tone. It was the most they'd heard come out of Aidan's mouth in the past couple moons, and for all that Mikael didn't really understand Shahi, the intent was obvious enough.

"They don't like to do the blood-rites anymore," Mandric said under the fighting. "They used to do it for power, since the Shahi gift comes in two sorts: channeller and focus. The channellers can harness more energy, while the focus can use that energy for a more powerful touch. In the past, they'd bind a channeller to a focus to amplify the potential of them both." He smiled slightly. "The Gold, the Shahi Queen, was an infamous focus. If she was fed too much energy, she had a tendency to blow things up."

"And Shahi magic is all about control," Soren said, always the strategian. "They broke it up into their song-lines to keep any one person from getting too much access to it. If they don't bind anyone anymore, then they'll prevent any amplified mages."

Comprehension suddenly hit Mikael; Soren had been right, in all of it. "Which is why you sent us here, because if anyone can figure out how to deal with a bond, it would be them." He nodded toward Aidan. "Is he bound to someone?"

Mandric concentrated, obviously trying to follow the flow of conversation. "He was," he said finally. "He'd bound himself to a channeller. Tai wasn't happy, so he broke the bond and they sent the other boy off to another hirhai."

Something froze in Mikael's guts. "So there are ways to… break the bond?" Katjin's grip on him tightened. "We're leaving now. Otherwise—" Katjin didn't need to say anymore. Mandric obviously got the gist.

Mandric studied them for a moment, as if considering something. "The snows begin soon—may already be in some of the highest passes," he said in an off-hand manner. "Might be a good idea to pack. I risked enough attempting a crossing at this time of year."

Soren snorted. "Pack what? We're ready to go."

Mandric's sudden laughter actually interrupted the fight going on in the corner between Tai and Aidan. "The boys are ready," he said, when Tai glared at him. "I'll take them now. Nolan will be glad to have them home."

Where exactly that home was, Mikael wasn't sure, but he could feel Katjin's excitement building. It would be nice to see Apa again, even if it wasn't under the best of circumstances.

"Wait—no! They can't leave." Tai held his hands up, as if to try and stop them. "We need them."

Soren stepped in front of Katjin and Mikael, casually leaning against the stick he'd taken to carrying.

"And they need to do this," Mandric said slowly, his voice bleak. "Ancestors know we can't stop them, even if we tried." He turned away from Tai. "Aidan."

Aidan looked up, rattling off a quick stream of Shahi.

"Go pack," was Mandric's only response.

With a wide grin, the Shahi boy held up the small pack he'd hidden behind his back.

Katjin's eyes almost bulged out of his head.

It would be an interesting trip over the pass.

Chapter Six

"Okay, you neglected to mention the cold," Mikael said, teeth chattering. The climb back over the mountains seemed a little easier, maybe because he and Katjin didn't need to cling to each other with every step. Just as they'd promised Tai, they practiced their control every day; they had to, trying to navigate the narrow trails that cut through the mountains. That didn't mean that the trails were any less lethal than they had been the first time. Mikael still stumbled over the uneven, rocky footing, focusing all of his attention on where he placed his feet so that he wouldn't be reminded of how narrow the trail was, or how steep the drop-off. The valleys that they looked into from the trail heights were dizzyingly-beautiful, but this high above the tree-line, the jumble of rocky shards and jagged cliffs that led down to the valleys were more than enough to remind Mikael of the danger.

Mandric gave him a surprised look. "I did mention the snow, right?" He pushed Mikael closer to the fire. "Cheer up, lad. We're almost up and over."

It was fall, which meant 'we really shouldn't be attempting this crossing' to people who weren't crazy. So far, the only snow they'd seen was up on the peaks, but that didn't mean it wasn't waiting for them higher up. According to Mandric, they had another day's walk before they got to the pass, and then it was downhill into the Highlands from there. They would regroup in the Highlands and then head out to the camp where Katjin's family was being held, and from there...

From there, they took down the Empire.

While they still wore their Clan robes, Tai had also gifted them with woolen breeks and shirts to go under their robes. The wool had been woven with rabbit fur, making it extra warm. Mikael had put his as soon as they hit the mountains proper, not wanting to chance anything. Katjin and Soren soon followed suit, and even Aidan was showing signs of chill by the third day. The freezing mountain air made for incredible views that Mikael hadn't quite appreciated, the first time they came over the pass. Now, though, he almost regretted leaving.

Then Katjin or Soren would wave a stick at him, and that nostalgic feeling would go away.

They camped each night in whatever hollow Mandric could find, all huddled into the small yer that Mandric brought with him. Katjin hadn't cried tears of relief at the sight of the yer, but Mikael did occasionally catch his bonded stroking the woven goat-hair, rubbing his nose against it as if he couldn't live without the dusty animal smell.

The mountains, while walling them in as they moved up and over the pass, seemed to loom over them. Mikael was surprised to find that he actually missed the trees. The sun was too bright, especially as it reflected off the snow on the peaks. The very light seemed like it was seeking them out, no longer as gentle as it had been, filtered through the canopy of the hirhai.

With the five of them crowded into all the floor-space that the yer offered, Mikael found himself often pinned between Katjin and the wall. While Soren had groaned continuously about being forced to share a sleeping space with them—again—Aidan at least seemed content to only watch Mikael from afar. It was disconcerting at times, very disconcerting, and it annoyed Katjin to no end.

"It's creepy," he said as they walked along the path.

"Maybe it's the bond," Mikael said, looking over his shoulder and not surprised to find Aidan watching them. Again. "Maybe he's jealous. Soren was, at first."

"Soren was randy and lonely," Katjin countered, a slightly squeamish look on his face. "As soon as we get back to camp—any camp—we're looking for a new friend for Soren."

Mikael turned his eyes toward Soren, at the back of the pack. Katjin's cousin was scanning the skies for something, though for what, Mikael couldn't even hazard a guess. Soren was decent looking, if you liked your fellas tall and strong and self-assured enough that they made even the most vulnerable feel safe. "What about Aidan?"

Katjin snorted. "Good one." Then he waited, probably for Mikael to finish the joke. "Aidan? And Soren?" The mere thought seemed to boggle Katjin's mind.

Mikael shrugged. "It would get Aidan off our backs, and it might lighten Soren up a little bit."

At that, Katjin looked thoughtful. "Maybe…"

"Hey, what are you two whispering about?" Soren called ahead. "You're falling behind!"

Mikael turned around, surprised to find Aidan and Mandric ten lengths or more ahead of them. Beyond them was…

"Snow?" Mikael ran past Mandric and Aidan toward

the glittering white. He could hear Katjin at his heels, hard pressed to keep up. "Kat, it's snow!"

The narrow valley they were climbing through suddenly opened into a round bowl, filled with what had to be snow. Mikael poked at it with one careful finger, delighted to feel the cold flakes crunching between his fingers. "Fresh snow, too!" he crowed. He grabbed his walking stick from where it hung on his pack and prodded the snow. It looked to be about knee-deep, which meant it was perfect for snow birds. "Katjin, c'mon!" He turned around and let himself fall backward into the frozen embrace of the snow. He moved his arms and legs in wide-sweeping arcs, pushing the snow aside. He could feel the wet seeping in past his robe, but didn't care. It was snow, and he hadn't seen snow in... well, he couldn't remember how long. Stoneridge never got a lot, but the country house did.

"Snow birds, eh, lad?" Mandric said, grinning down at Mikael. "I haven't made one of them in quite a long time." Then his face darkened. "If there's snow here, though, that means it'll be rough-going over the pass."

Soren and Katjin hung back at the edge of the snow field. When Mikael thought about it, he could feel the familiar twinges of nausea and headache starting up again. Damn it. He pulled himself out of the snow and loped over to Katjin, the ache fading with each step. If he didn't pay attention to it, it seemed that he could stretch the bond between the two of them much further than when he thought about it. If he had to go through life humming under his breath, he'd do it, if only to be able to use the privy alone for the first time in a long time.

"What's wrong?" he asked, grinning at Katjin. "Don't you like snow?" Both Katjin and Soren were looking at the snow with something like distaste on their faces. "It's just frozen water. Don't you get snow on the plains?" The plains stretched so much higher and further north than the Lowlands, even Stoneridge, that he would've thought Katjin saw snow every winter.

"Not in Winter Camp," Soren said, poking at the snow field with one toe. "Up in the high camps, aye, but we always take the herds south to avoid the snow. It's too hard to feed them and keep them warm up there."

Katjin knelt down, removed one glove and patted the snow lightly. "I've seen it," he said, poking his fingers deeper into the snow. "We'd see it from the road sometimes, but Apa never wanted to stop."

Mandric laughed. "Ask your apa about the winter he spent in the Highlands, little Kat. That'll explain your apa's distaste for snow."

Katjin was so absorbed in the snow that he actually forgot to scowl at Mandric's use of the nickname. "What's this snow bird thing?" he asked, looking up at Mikael. "It doesn't look like a bird."

Mikael rolled his eyes. His bonded was a little too literal sometimes. "Here, I'll show you." He grabbed Katjin by the hand, positioned him with his back to the snow, and then pushed him in. Katjin yelped in surprise, and then even louder as he sank down into the snow pack.

"It's cold!" he shrieked, flailing about for a minute.

"No, dumbnut, not like that," Mikael said, flopping on top of Katjin. He moved Katjin's arms and legs in the slow, sweeping arcs that you needed to create the snow bird. "See? Your legs create the tail, and your arms create the wings."

"Looks like a girl wearing a skirt," Soren remarked, watching them with an amused look on his face. Mikael stuck his tongue out at Soren in response.

Before Mikael could say anything else, though, he heard a whoop and a crash as another body plunged into the snow next to him and Katjin. Aidan grinned at him, yellow eyes bright, and he flung his arms and legs out to make a snow bird of his own.

"Bird," Aidan said proudly, sitting up in the snow.

Mikael looked at Katjin, who was still lying back in the snow. Katjin's green eyes stared solemnly back. "Bird," he echoed. Something in those green eyes made Mikael lean in, press his nose against Katjin's, his lips—

He could feel the eyes on his back, heard Soren groaning as he usually did whenever he caught Mikael and Katjin at 'it,' as he called it. Katjin's eyes widened slightly, as it occurred to Katjin too that they had an audience.

"Ancestors," Katjin muttered, his face going red. "Um, Mik, maybe you better get up."

Someone coughed behind them. Mikael slid to his knees, reaching out a hand to haul Katjin up. Katjin gave him a thankful grin, still blushing fiercely. While the red didn't show quite as much on Katjin's tanned cheeks, it was still evident enough. He knew his own face had to be burning.

"Help. Aye?" Aidan asked, holding out his own hand. The Shahi looked flushed as well. Of course, the one emotion Mikael could actually read off Aidan would have to be that...

Without looking back at Katjin, Mikael held out a gloved hand to Aidan. Their hands met, and even Katjin had to feel the spark that jumped between them. As quick as he could, he hauled Aidan's light weight out of the snow.

"Should probably get going, aye, Mandric?" Mikael said, hurrying back toward Mandric without a second glance.

Heart Song

***

The snow made it slow-going. Walking sticks came out, and Mikael was glad more than once that he had use of both hands on this trip. The extra woolen layers definitely helped, as did the oiled leather cloaks that Mandric produced for them out of his bottomless pack. As their feet crunched endlessly over snowdrift after snowdrift, though, constantly slipping in the melting ice, Mikael wondered if there wasn't an easier way.

"The Empire came by ship, aye?" he asked Aidan, who marched just in front of him.

Aidan looked back, moving over the snow almost as easily as Mandric did. Though they didn't seem to have snow down in the Shahi forests, Mikael supposed that a lifetime of running across rain-slicked branches would probably be good practice for slippery snow.

"Empire, ship?" Aidan's face screwed up in concentration. He mouthed the words several times. "Ship. Aye, to harbor."

If there was a sea route around the mountains, why didn't they just take that? There had to be some kind of bay or harbor on the south side of the mountains that they could safely sail into.

"It's not that easy, lad," Mandric said, breaking into Mikael's thoughts. "It's days and days of sailing before you come to safe harbor, and you can bet that the Empire knows it. I'm sure that, as much as they would love to extend up through the mountains and into the fertile Shahi valleys again, it won't happen, just because of the dangers of sailing that coast."

Aidan rattled something off to Mandric in Shahi. Mikael thought he caught a word that sounded like boat and city, but wasn't sure.

"The lad says that, the reason the Cityfolk settled where they did was because that was where their ship wrecked. They weren't necessarily looking to settle there," Mandric translated as they huffed their way over the pass. "They apparently wanted to go north, to the warmer lands. Where Empirefolk came from, it was colder than anything. That's why our folk—Highland and Horse Clan—settled where they did in the lea of the mountains."

"And why Stoneridge always got the snow, where you might not have," Mikael added. "But we'll leave all this behind soon, won't we?"

Mandric nodded. "This is the top of the pass, right here."

The way down was almost anticlimactic. Mikael's knees and thighs hurt from the sheer pressure on them, supporting his weight and keeping him from falling his way down the mountain, but it was nothing compared to the endless toil up. It was almost a relief to leave all that green behind, settling back into the alpine scrublands that covered this side of the Highlands.

"We're back," he said as they settled into camp that night. Mandric estimated only a couple more days before they came to an actual Highlandfolk camp.

"Can you smell the difference in the air?" Katjin asked, nose wrinkling. "It's not so... green, I guess."

There was a damp smell about them, but Mikael figured it was them more than the air itself. "The mountains keep the dry air on this side, I suppose," he said, relaxing next to Katjin by the fire. They still had another day or so of snow, but it was patchier here than on the Shahi side of the mountains. "Another couple days, and we'll have our own yer again." He actually missed the small yer they'd shared in the valley—was it even a moon ago? "Mandric snores."

Katjin laughed. "So does Aidan. Wonder what Soren'll think of that." They both looked at where Soren and Aidan sat, discussing something with Mandric as intermediary.

"No. Not," Aidan said, waving his hand at Soren to be quiet. "Horse Clan, aye?" His brows furrowed in concentration as he searched for the words. "Brother—brother?—with Highlandfolk." He touched his tongue. "Same. Same. Aye?"

Mikael looked at Katjin. "Is that why I can understand what Mandric says with no problem? Because Highlandtongue is the same as Clantongue?"

Katjin shrugged. "No one ever says much about Highlandfolk, so I never knew until Soren brought the Highlandfolk into the big rescue effort." He made a face in Soren's direction. "What Soren was thinking, bringing them into this..."

Mik touched Katjin's hand. "Saved me, didn't it?" he said quietly, staring at Mandric's profile, so like Katjin and Soren's. "Aye, they sent us to the Shahi demons, but they helped more than they had to. They didn't have to come out of their hills to help us."

"Aye, they did," Katjin answered with a slight smile. "Soren sang the aiding song at them."

Their hands found each other, winding tight together. "Mother only taught that to me and Em," Mikael said, not sure why he was sharing that with Katjin, or why he hadn't before. "Em didn't mind me too much—didn't blame me too much for us leaving Stoneridge. I don't know if she and my other sisters even realized I wasn't branded. Mother always tried to keep me separated from them—from anyone, really. I think I had a nurse once, but she left before I could really remember."

He swallowed, hoping that she was safe somewhere. For all their faults, his mother and father had tried their best. Mother had her moments of warmth, though they were few and far between, almost as if she was afraid to get too close. One of those moments had been when she taught him and Emera the aiding song. "She used to say that, if you listened close enough, you could hear someone's heart-song. That's what 'paths were listening for, though the Empire had forgotten that. The 'pathing gifts weren't meant to guard and read secrets, they were meant to help. To read someone's heart-song to see how you could best help them."

Katjin nodded. "A 'path came to help my ama," he said, as if he suddenly remembered. "Ama was pregnant, and the baby wouldn't come. The baby protested, I think the 'path said. I remember the 'path talking and talking to someone that none of us could see, crooning to the baby and begging it to let Ama go, to be born." He swallowed. "But the 'path wasn't able to, and the baby and Ama died."

"So there's some good to 'paths," Mikael said, wondering where the Empire had gone wrong. "We just have to find it again, I suppose."

"Heart song," Katjin mused. "I like the sound of that." He brought Mikael's hand up to his heart, so that Mikael could feel the beat. "That's my heart song." And for a moment, it beat exactly in time with Mikael's.

Chapter Seven

He could see the black-and-white tents gathered in a circle around a central fire. He even thought he heard a familiar whinny as they descended into the valley that engulfed the camp. The figure standing in front of what was obviously a Clan yer noticed them probably at the same moment they noticed him.

"Apa!" Katjin tore away from Mikael, rushing at his father. Mikael followed at a more sedate pace, humming to himself. Katjin didn't need the worry or the pain right now, even if they had gotten better at the whole distance thing. He was still careful to keep himself within a stride of Katjin, though, just to be on the safe side.

"Kat!" Apa grabbed his son, hugging him tight. He looked over Katjin's shoulder, as if he was searching for someone. To Mikael's surprise, Apa's eyes actually lit up when they landed on him. "Mikael, c'mon." There was a brief, hard hug for Mikael too, one that he tried not to linger in for too long. Apa was a wash of emotions, a mess of swirling guilt and dread and such utter happiness that it was almost too much.

As if Katjin sensed Mikael pushing away, he dropped his arms from around Apa and stood back a step, carefully in line with Mikael. "Maybe the Shahi weren't so bad after all," Katjin said, the quiet pride obvious in his voice as they stood without touching.

Apa's eyes widened. "I didn't think— That is, Tai is good at loosening bonds, but I didn't think he would get results this quick." Apa touched Katjin's face, where the faded yellow bruise was still visible on one cheekbone. "This, though…"

"One of Tai's tactics," Mikael said, scowling. "He had this stick, and—"

Apa groaned. "Sometimes I think Tai might take it a little too seriously." He looked past them. "Isn't that Tai's son?" He sounded surprised, then gave Katjin a stern look. "Did he follow you home?"

Katjin scowled. "I didn't know that the goat herd belonged to that Salt River clan," he muttered. "Besides, he likes Mik better anyway."

Mikael heard a neighing come from beyond the row of yer, and suddenly realized who it was. Katjin's eyes widened. "Apa—"

Apa nodded. "Go to her, Kat. She's all but wasted away since you went over the mountain."

Without a second glance, Katjin raced off. Mikael trotted behind him, doing his best to keep up. He hadn't thought that Clan horses were that devoted to their masters. Stars knew that his pony could've cared less if anything happened to him.

"It's because they're our children," Apa said, suddenly at Mikael's elbow. He loped along next to Mikael as if it was the most natural thing in the world. "We bring them into our yer in winter and we'll sacrifice anything we can to keep them healthy and well-fed." He smiled slightly. "You'll never see a starving colt or child on the plains. Adults would rather go without than do anything to damage their future." He shook his head. "The Empire doesn't seem to understand that though. It isn't the first time they've underestimated us."

Shanti, Katjin's chestnut mare, was grazing not far beyond the last yer. To Mikael's surprise, she was actually hobbled.

"We had to," Apa called, when Katjin shot him an accusing look. "Otherwise she would've tried to go over the mountain after you."

Shanti whinnied fiercely, straining to break the hobbles. Before she could do any damage, Katjin and Mikael rushed toward her. Katjin unfastened the buckle at her neck while Mikael unlaced the hobble that went between her front hooves, catching at the fetlock. Once she was free, Shanti nosed over every inch of Katjin, as if to make sure he was safe. Once she was satisfied, she turned to Mikael and did the same thing, snuffling horse breath all over his face and shoulders and hair. She chewed at a loose strand of blond hair idly before stepping back and neighing at him. Out of instinct, he threw his arms around her neck, breathing in her warm, horsey scent. He hadn't imagined how much he'd miss horses, but Shanti had saved his life on several occasions.

"You know she'll be insulted," Katjin said in a low voice. "Once she realizes you'll be riding your own horse."

Mikael's jaw dropped. "Think we can do that?" There was something nice about sitting behind Katjin, pressed up against his body's warmth as they rode, but he knew they'd both grown a little in the past few moons. It wouldn't be fair to make Shanti carry both of them, especially if they had any more daring escapes they needed to make.

Someone behind them snorted. "Don't see why not," Soren said, giving Shanti his own pat. "As long as the horses don't mind walking abreast and within about a half a stride of each other."

Katjin turned around to look at Apa. "Could we?" he asked, the longing clear in his voice. He looked back at Mikael apologetically. "Not that I'm kicking you off my horse, but—"

Mikael laughed. "Much as I love you, Kat, I do want to do some things on my own again."

And then he stopped. Katjin stopped, staring at him, though no one else seemed to notice.

"That is—" Mikael coughed. "It's been a while since I've ridden by myself."

Katjin seemed oddly quiet that night. They sat around the campfire. Shanti, now off her lead, hovered just out of range of the circle, constantly watching him and Mikael. Aidan had almost run her off earlier, when he caught the two of them playing a chasing game with Shanti.

It seemed like a good idea at the time. Shanti had refused to let them out of her sight once she realized they weren't going anywhere, so Katjin and Mikael had taken to chasing her around the pasturing area. It was a good test of their range as they ran about, hand in hand, breaking only to confuse Shanti once she got too close. But apparently someone didn't quite explain the game to Aidan, because as soon as Shanti decided to play back, charging Mikael at a fast canter, the Shahi decided to step in.

THUD!

"Ow!" Aidan's body slammed into Mikael's, knocking him out of the way of Shanti's thundering hooves.

There was another thump as Katjin tackled Aidan, knocking him off Mik. "You stupid demon, what the hell are you doing?" Katjin all but screamed in Aidan's ear, hands around Aidan's neck.

"Horse!" Aidan yelled right back. He rolled Katjin, gripping Katjin's neck and thudding Katjin's head into the ground with each word. "Horse attack, aye? Hit Mikael. Aye, I saved!" he spat.

Then Katjin's fist connected with Aidan's chin.

Mikael dove in, trying to pry Katjin off Aidan. "He didn't mean it! C'mon, Kat, think!"

They rolled off Aidan, staring at each other.

"Why're you defending him? He your new bonded now?" Katjin sneered, trying to dominate Mikael.

"Maybe it's better him than you," Mikael shouted back, so tempted to shove every bit of anger and dread right back down Katjin's throat til he choked on it. "What's the matter with you?" He pushed Katjin off, struggling to his feet.

"I just…" Katjin sat up, staring at Mikael. Mik could see a yellowish bruise darkening around Katjin's right eye, making a nice match for the other fading bruise on his face. "I don't understand you anymore."

Mikael actually stopped and stared. "Why, because of Aidan?" He ran his hand through his hair in frustration, torn out of its tails while they wrestled on the ground. He was strangely happy to have the curls falling in his face again. It gave him something to hide behind, since Katjin could already read his heart better than anyone else.

Katjin stopped, faced Mikael. He leaned in close, til

they were almost nose to nose. Normally, that would be an invitation for a kiss, but not now. Even a non-'path could read this.

"Is it because of Aidan?" Katjin repeated quietly. "Is that why you wanted to stay in the hirhai?"

Mikael shook his head quickly. "Kat, you know I—" That was the problem, though. They'd never really talked about it, definitely never mentioned those words that most people seemed to take for granted. Even though Mikael knew how strong Katjin felt and how much he himself cared, sometimes he wondered if it was because of their blood bond, or if it was something that came from inside themselves.

"I'm just tired, aye? Tired of the fight, tired of shielding, tired of—" He shook his head again, not knowing what else to do. "Tired of not being able to live."

Katjin dropped his eyes, stood up and turned away. "And this isn't living? Finding my family—finding *your* family—and trying to take down the Empire? That's not worth it?"

He stood and caught at Katjin's hands, dragging his bonded back to face him. "Kat..." How could he admit that he wasn't even sure if he wanted his family to be found? That it was easier to face the possibility that they might have escaped alive somewhere than admit that they were dead, or worse, because of him? It was bad enough that an entire camp full of Clanfolk that he'd never even consciously met paid a price because of what he was. He didn't want that to happen to more people within the Empire. Not even when they were so close to saving those very Clanfolk he'd condemned.

Katjin backed away, biting his lip. Mikael followed the careful step that he needed to keep the nausea at bay.

"No, I know. I understand. You want to be free." And before Mikael could take another step forward, Katjin hurried away, back to the camp. "Maybe it's time we tried to be free!"

He fell to his knees, head pounding, his stomach rushing somewhere north of his throat until it felt like he would hurl all over the grass. The world spun, but he fought back, trying to steady his breathing. In and out, just the way Tai taught him. In and out, centering himself, steadying himself. One step back, one step forward, block, slip—just like the steps of all the stick-fighting work that Tai had them do.

They had been instructed in staves as a way to get rid of all that extra energy. Tai thought that, if they were tired enough, they wouldn't project so much. That if they learned to work in unison, mirroring each other stock-fighting, it would help with their control and teach them to focus so that they could work together. But their rhythm was off. Their rhythm had been off from the beginning. Katjin was trying to sing one song, and Mikael's heart was in another, and with Katjin being off-key, Mik wondered why he had to be the one to adapt to what Katjin couldn't sing. It should be the other way around, since he was the heart-sense. He was the one who got them into this mess. He was the reason why they had to go and rescue Katjin's family, since Katjin's family had at least given a damn about him.

Maybe that was it. He knew there was a certain amount of jealousy involved, but he hadn't thought it was so serious. His family left him, while Katjin's family had done their best to give him a chance to live. Aye, they had sent him off into the hinterlands of the plains with a kid his own age and Soren for protection, but they hadn't left him to die the way his own family had. Clanfolk were all about Clan and lived only for Clan. His own father had tried so hard to do what he thought was best for Mikael, but Mikael couldn't help but wonder if it was all a mistake, if it wouldn't have been better as an Empire 'path, not knowing the difference in the first place.

Apa had dragged him back to the camp not long after Katjin stormed off, not saying anything. All through supper, Katjin hadn't uttered a word of apology or otherwise, even though he had maintained the distance they needed for their bond.

"Dissent's growing," Apa was saying, mostly talking to Mandric and Soren, their strategians. "I hear it everywhere now. Even in the city streets, in the Lowlands and on the coast. While Lowlanders might not understand what happened in the Clan lands, they still know that a trust was violated—moreso than it ever had before."

"My father used to mention it, when he thought I wasn't listening," Mikael spoke up, since Katjin wasn't going to pay attention. "He used to say that all it would take was one incident to incite the whole country."

Mandric looked thoughtful. "Well, you have your incident. Word's spread," he said. "Leaked out from the plains and into the Lowlands about what happened to your camp."

That sparked something in Katjin. "People know?" Katjin asked, blinking. "I thought that the Empire controlled every thought that came and went across the Lowlands." He wasn't looking at Mikael, but Mik knew the comment was directed at him.

"Not everyone buys into the Empire's philosophy." Mikael did his best not to sneer. "Father would've sold me to the Empire if he believed in all that shite." Not that what he did do was arguably any better…

"Your apa also did his best to damn an entire camp of innocent people," Katjin shot back, the first signs of emotions lighting up his face.

"Lads!" Apa barked. "None of that. If you want to be a part of this, then you have to act like the adults you want to be treated as. That means cooperation with us and with each other. If you can't cooperate, then, well…" He trailed off, then turned to Soren. "If we find their camp, do you think you can infiltrate?"

Soren nodded, eyes lighting up with a fire that Mikael hadn't seen in a long time. Soren needed to be focused on something, and since he wasn't directly responsible for Mik and Katjin anymore, this seemed like a good enough cause to take its place. That made Mikael feel better, since he never wanted to be anyone's purpose in life. "They might not buy me waving a white flag at them, but I'm sure they'd be plenty happy to take me prisoner." He grinned. "Being a blood traitor and all." The grin grew bitter. "Bastards and blood-traitors that they are."

Apa snorted. "Recognized a couple of the cavalry, did you?"

"You can't send him alone, though, Nolan," Mandric protested. "If something goes wrong, if we lose him—it's not worth the price. Especially if the 'paths get to him."

"I'm not a babe!" Soren said with a scowl. He waved at Mikael and Katjin. "I kept those two idiots alive for moons. I should be able to handle this."

Mandric smiled slightly. "We'll see, lad."

"Send Aidan with Soren," Katjin spoke up, not looking at Mikael. "He's got magic. He can protect Soren."

Before Soren could protest, Apa cut in. "That's a good point, Kat. If Aidan could alert us somehow…" He turned to Aidan. "Would you go with Soren, let us know when they capture him?"

Aidan stared at Apa, mouthing the words over and over until they made sense. Then, he turned to Mikael, the request for help obvious in his eyes.

"Go with Soren," Mikael repeated. "Hide, like we did from the moah." He put his arms up in front of his face, peering through his hands at Aidan.

"Hide, from moah," Aidan repeated. "Go with Soren. Hide, from moah." His yellow eyes lit up. "From moah! Hide."

"You let us know when they take Soren?" Mikael reached out his arm, loping it around Soren's neck and pretending to drag him off. "This happens, you shoot?" He pointed his finger up in the air, freeing his other hand to make like sparks were coming off his splayed fingers.

Aidan nodded, obviously understanding. He grinned. "Not guard with Soren. Send them a message, aye?" He looked at Mikael for confirmation. "I. Send message to Apa, aye? I watch." He put his hand up to his eyes, mimicking sentry duty on the camp. "You're hurt, aye? I send message."

"Back-up," Apa said. "We don't doubt your abilities, Soren. Or any of you. But I don't want to send any of you lads out alone. If Aidan could send us a message somehow, that would probably be the best way." He turned his head toward Mikael. "I don't suppose…"

Mikael shook his head. "That's more of a thought-sense thing. I can definitely track Soren, but that's because we've done it before, with Tai in the hirhai. Especially with Katjin with me. Aidan…" He shrugged. "Might be more of a problem, since I can't read him for anything."

Apa looked thoughtful. "Can you read the absence of

his emotions? If his shield is that good?"

Mikael looked at Katjin, who shrugged. "We can practice with it," Katjin said. "What about energy, though? Could we track him through the energy he uses? Mik tapped into that, back with the Shahi."

Fighting off a shudder at the memory of the fire, Mikael said, "Could try that too." He wasn't sure how good an idea that was, considering what had happened last time, but time was short, and they couldn't exactly take their time anymore. "Aidan, can you go… somewhere else?" He waved his hand vaguely in the direction of away. "I want to track you through your magic."

Again, that fierce look of concentration from Aidan as he muttered under his breath. Then he grinned. "Aye, aye."

"Think it'll work?" Katjin muttered as Mikael closed his eyes.

Mikael shrugged. "Can't hurt, and it would make our lives easier." He heard the usual rustling about the fire and some voices, but not much more than that. The background noise more than sufficiently covered whatever sounds Aidan might've made, and since Aidan already moved as silently as Soren, it would make the test all the more challenging. "Think he's ready?"

"Ready." Then he heard Katjin call out, "Aidan, show us some magic!"

Whatever it was, it was as quiet as Aidan's footfalls. Mikael tried to sort through the emotions around him, blocking out the unimportant ones. Katjin's concentration beside him was immediately evident, and not necessary. As he tried to focus on anything unusual, any extra effort that didn't seem as familiar as Mandric, Apa or Soren, he caught something.

It was like fire, hot to the touch and intoxicating. The heady rush of it sent his head into a spin, almost as much as that first touch after the blood-binding ceremony had. There was a certain exultation to it, like it was something that mere mortals weren't supposed to know. Maybe that's how the Shahi had gotten their reputation as demons, if that's what using magic felt like.

He stood up, wavering a bit as the ecstasy surrounded him. Katjin's hand on his elbow steadied him as he slowly turned in a circle, tasting each direction for that current. It reminded him of the smell of lightning in the air, just before a storm.

It took him two or three rotations, but then he caught it. Dragging Katjin along behind him, he raced toward it, trusting that Katjin's eyes and arms would guide him around any obstacles. They sped across the camp, heading up a slight incline. The hair stood up on the back of his neck and arms as they got closer and closer until Mikael could almost feel it rushing through his veins, liquid fire and quicksilver, potent as that moonshine that the Clanfolk called their aisrag.

Hands clamped down on his arms, but the touch was unfamiliar. He struggled, because they burned white hot, the image of the figure almost burning itself into his eyelids. "Wha—" he croaked, as the hands let him go.

"You found me." Aidan's voice was soft, not just surprised but almost shocked. "Aye. With magic."

He opened his eyes, an outline of white-hot power still crackling around Aidan. Turning to look over his shoulder, even Katjin seemed to glow with the same fierce fireflicker light.

"You okay?" Katjin asked, warm concern wrapping around Mikael like a blanket. The fuzziness of the feeling helped tame the edge of the power that still coursed through him, bringing the earth back from that frighteningly-sharp clarity that everything had burned with.

Mikael nodded, letting the gray take him. "Okay," his voice croaked again, and then he collapsed against Katjin's shoulder.

"…all your fault," he heard Katjin yelling at someone, probably Soren, since Katjin liked to yell at Soren.

"He tracked!" That was Aidan's voice, which meant the Shahi was taking the brunt of Katjin's anger.

"Aye, he tracked, and then he glowed, and then he passed out. Explain that!" Katjin snapped back.

Mikael opened his eyes blearily, not surprised to find Aidan waving his hand at Katjin, his favorite gesture for making people be quiet.

"Energy. Magic, the waves, the…" Aidan waved at someone else, speaking rapidly in Shahi.

"Wasn't Aidan, lad," Mandric spoke up. "It was overload, best I can tell. Aidan's not a channeller, so he wasn't aware that he was giving off that much energy. Heart-senses must absorb energy along the same pathways that the Shahi do their magic. Your Mik just got a little fried is all."

"Just a little…" Katjin's jaw dropped. He fell to his knees next to Mikael. "You're not fried, are you?" he asked, worry almost overwhelming Mikael.

"Not fried, maybe crispy," Mikael said, his voice sounding like a frog's. His throat burned at the mere attempt to talk. "Starless hells."

Katjin's arm slid behind Mikael's shoulders, helping him up. Mikael noticed that they were back in the yer again. They seemed to spend a lot of time waking up there after blacking out. He wondered if it was even the same yer.

"You fainted with the overload. That's probably something we should've thought of," Apa said, kneeling on the other side of Mikael. "Kat, feel his forehead. Is he clammy? Feverish?"

Katjin's hand felt cool on his head. The general fuzziness wore off a little at the touch. Mikael leaned into the hand, glad of the calming effect the skin-to-skin contact seemed to have. Stars, if he and Katjin actually managed full skin-on-skin...

"Is he blacking out again?" Apa asked.

"No, Apa, he..." Even from Katjin's shoulder, Mikael could see the blush spreading over his bonded's neck and cheeks. "I think he's fine, not fried at all." That was punctuated with a glare at Aidan, who looked miserable.

"Not. My. Fault. Aye," Aidan said flatly before stalking off out the yer.

Mikael looked at Apa and Mandric. "So I got his energy? Thought that required magic 'pathy or something."

Mandric looked thoughtful. "The Shahi have always treated the 'pathing gifts and magic gifts as separate, lad. No one ever thought to consider that they might use the same mental pathways. Or emotional ones." He gave Mikael a small smile. "Felt the rush, aye?"

Eyed wide, Mikael nodded frantically. This was more than the power he'd accidentally tapped when he got angry at Tai—purer, brighter, more tantalizing. He swallowed. This could get dangerous. "It was like..." He shook his head.

"Aisrag," Katjin finished. "Like swallowing lightning." He made a face. "And then, when I touched Mik, he shocked me. We even saw little sparks." His dark brown hair was still standing on end, even more so than usual.

Apa turned to Mandric. "Did Tai ever mention why he broke Aidan's bond?"

Mandric scratched his chin. "Not in so many words. From what I'd gathered, it wasn't because the Tai didn't like the other boy—in fact, I think Tai'd enjoyed the idea of him as a son. Knowing Tai, though, he was probably just afraid of what might happen as a result." He scowled. "I'm surprised he didn't attempt it on our two."

Mikael looked at Katjin, who seemed equally stunned by that offhand remark.

"Babies?" Katjin asked in an innocent voice, once he'd regained his composure. Apa just snorted at the remark.

Ignoring it as well, Mandric continued. "Probably because he wanted to put some limits on the lad's power. Blood bonds amplify magic potential to almost unbelievable levels. Aidan wasn't even these two's age when they bonded. Since Tai knows full well what the Empire could do with someone like a bonded mage pair in their hands, he was probably wisest to break it when he did."

Mikael exchanged a look with Katjin. "Might explain why he's so obsessed with Mik," Katjin said. "If breaking the bond was as horrible as it sounds…" He shuddered.

"Darkest—" Mikael hadn't even thought about that. "Is it like our bond?"

Mandric shrugged. "I don't know, lad. It's not something the Shahi are that fond of discussing with outsiders, even blood kin. I'm surprised Tai was willing to work with you at all. He's been so obsessed over the years with destroying the threat of the Empire, once and for all, that I think the opportunity that you brought was more than enough to break those prejudices."

"Damn it, I can't start feeling sorry for him," Katjin muttered. "But that must've hurt so much." His grip on Mikael tightened. "How can you break something like this without destroying someone?"

Apa nodded toward Mandric. "I haven't seen Aidan since he was small, but from what others have said, the boy was broken for moons after they separated him." He looked bleak. "I'm not entirely sure the other boy survived."

"Which is one more reason why we have to keep you two out of the hands of the Empire." Mandric's voice was emphatic. "We can't lose you."

"Because of how you can use us, and what we can do? Since no one else seems able to do it?" Mikael asked sourly.

Apa looked hurt. "Lad, do you not realize?" He knelt down, cupping Mikael's face in one bare hand, well aware of what that affect would have. Mikael had to bite his lip to counteract the brief pain. "You mean the world to us, just as much as Little Kat here. You're Clan."

Looking up at Katjin, Mikael saw his bonded nodding. "Can't separate us except by force," he said, his voice thick with emotion.

"The day will come, lads," Mandric warned. "Just 'ware that fact."

"And in the mean time," Apa added, "we might have an effective tracking method for Soren and Aidan."

As Mandric and Apa both headed off, Mikael turned to Katjin. "You were being a shite today," he said flatly, tired of dancing around it. "I'm not picking Aidan, and I wish you'd get that through your thick head."

Katjin had the decency to both look and feel ashamed, almost mortified by his own behavior. "I didn't—" He shook his head, obviously hearing the whinging even in his own voice. "I acted like a kid, and that's why Apa treats me like a kid," he said finally. His green eyes sought Mikael's. "I need to act like an adult, but to do that, I have to take responsibility for myself, which is what I think Apa was trying to tell me all along."

Mikael touched Katjin's cheek lightly, tracing the bruises. "We can't keep beating it into your skull, otherwise you're going to look like a rainbow hit you in the face."

Snorting, Katjin ducked his head. "Well, if that's what it takes to teach me my lesson…"

Mikael grinned. "I'm sure Soren would be happy to help me out there." He tipped Katjin's face up, giving him a serious look. "So we're good again? No more fights about Aidan?"

Katjin nodded. "No more fights about Aidan. Other things, though…"

With a laugh, Mikael hooked an arm around Katjin's neck and kissed him. "Agreed."

"Again," Apa said softly, watching Katjin and Mikael go through their paces. Katjin was perched on Shanti's back, while Mikael rode as close as possible to his side on his own horse, Marae. Marae, named for the Shahi word for 'home,' was apparently half-sister or cousin or something to Shanti, but Katjin's mare only seemed to tolerate Marae's presence because Mikael and Katjin were there. Mikael wasn't sure when Katjin's horse started thinking of him in a proprietary fashion, but it didn't surprise him too much. Nothing did, these days.

"Figure eight," Katjin muttered as they set off together. It wasn't Mikael controlling Marae so much as Marae following Shanti's lead, somehow picking up on the fact that Mikael needed to be as close to Katjin as possible. Maybe it had been those three or four bad falls, when Shanti got too far out of Mikael's range with Katjin. Or that time that Shanti had almost run Marae down because Marae wasn't listening to Mikael's cues.

It was too bad that 'pathy didn't include animals. It was possible that there were heart-senses or thought-senses in the Empire that could speak with animals, but Mikael hadn't heard of any. If anyone would have such a gift, it would probably come from the plains anyway.

Their horses wheeled into a figure eight, loping slowly into one circle before switching lead and turning the other way. Mikael shifted his weight, moving his pelvis in slow circles with the movement of the lope. Riding on the glorified horse blanket that the Clanfolk called a saddle was still something to get used to. So was riding without a bridle. Apa and Soren had figured that it was easiest to find a horse who was content to follow Shanti's lead, allowing Mikael to concentrate on managing their bond, and Katjin to control the horses.

As soon as the horses segued into the next pattern, a cloverleaf, Mikael started to sing. It wasn't very loud, and Marae cocked one dark brown ear back at Mikael when he began, but it was enough. If he timed the beat of the song to the beat of the hooves, it gave him enough to occupy his mind that he didn't think about the bond. It rankled with him a little bit, since his mind had somehow absorbed the whole Shahi 'rhythm is wrong' thing. He had to go with what helped him most, though, and unfortunately, this was the kind of soothing rhythm he needed.

Thunder down, Lowland town
Fear the fire and plunder
When Clan rides across the sky
Bringing death and sunder
Fire down, Lowland town
Wooden walls to founder
When the Clan strikes again
Bringing death and sunder
Batten down, Lowland town
In the grassy yonder
Bar the gates in dire straits,
Protect from death and sunder

The tune was simple and repetitive, something every Lowlander child learned when they were small. For Mikael, it had been paired with the aiding song in most of his memories, making for an odd picture of the rampaging Clanfolk that used to ride down from their plains. The fact that he was riding on a Clan horse, about to rain death and sunder down on his own people, was almost too ironic for his mind to handle.

"Easy, Mik," Katjin hissed across the two horses at him. "The song. Just the song." Then Katjin's voice joined in, slightly high and slightly off-key, to the words.

Hoof beats roll a simple toll
Sending town to wander
Steal the children and the foals
Bringing death and sunder
Bar the gate, set the bait
Hunker in the cellar

Watch and wait til it's too late
Bringing death and sunder

That verse struck a little too close to home, reminding Mikael of those first fevered hours in the stone room, fingers covering every span of wall to try and find a window or some way *out*. Starless hells, how he hated the dark. If the cavalry ever did ride down on his home again—no matter who rode with them—he'd face them, weapon in hand, and bring them down.

Batten down, Lowland town
In the grassy yonder
Bar the gates in dire straits,
Protect from death and sunder

Chapter Eight

"It's Soren!" Katjin called as Soren's horse raced into camp. "And he's not happy." Even a non-'path could read the dark scowl on Soren's face.

"What happened?" Apa asked in a rush, racing over to Soren's horse.

"They moved the blasted camp!" Soren shouted, sliding off his horse. "And they've disappeared without a trace. Ancestors damn them!" He kicked at the grass. "Unless they've got mages or demons, they can't have moved that fast."

Mandric asked Aidan something in Shahi. The only response was a shaken head. "Aidan hasn't sensed anyone tapping into the magic currents," Mandric said. "He'd notice. His range is probably about what Mikael's—" He stopped. "Can we track 'em that way, Nolan? Use the lads?"

Apa hesitated before turning to Mikael and Katjin. "Is your range that good?" Apa asked, obviously trying not to be too hopeful. "We don't want to stretch you this early, not with the more crucial role coming later."

Katjin shot a look at Mikael, who shrugged. "We can try," Katjin said finally. "Besides, you can't send in Soren and Aidan if we don't know where they are."

Aidan squawked, as if he'd just thought of something. "Mandric! Glass, to see?" He rattled off another long phrase in Shahi, but this time, Mandric looked thoughtful.

"One of the song-lines that Aidan knows is what they call a scryer," Mandric said slowly. "Lets them look at something far away. Maybe we could use that to boost our 'path here, get a better estimate on how far away they moved the camp."

Mikael nodded, trying to stifle the excitement he could feel building through his link to Katjin. "It's possible," he said cautiously. "What does Aidan need to do this far-seeing thing?"

"Clothe," Aidan said, once Mandric asked him in Shahi. "Clothe with Meke or Febe?"

Katjin's eyes lit up. He ran off toward their yer so fast that Mikael couldn't even react. He came streaking back, gripping a scrap of blue cloth in his hands. "My robe. Meke made it. Would this help?" He thrust it at Aidan, who turned the blue cloth over in his hands, tracing the faint horse embroidery with light fingers.

"Horse," Aidan said quietly. "Horse from Meke?" He looked at Katjin, his eyes full of regret.

Katjin nodded. "My meke made it for me, at the beginning of summer." And they were coming into winter now. Darkest night, how many moons had it been?

Aidan looked at Mikael. "I go," he said simply. "You follow?"

Mikael wasn't entirely sure what that meant, but nodded. "I follow."

Another stream of Shahi from Aidan, and Mandric looked around frantically. "Do we have a map somewhere?" he asked Apa especially.

Apa's face brightened. "Believe it or not…" This time, it was Apa that raced off toward the yer, coming back bearing a thick scroll. He pushed a stack of papers off a nearby camp table and unrolled the scroll carefully. It was the clearest map Mikael had ever seen of the Empire, noting what looked like every seasonal camp of the Horse Clans, every Lowland town and village, and even the larger land holdings. With surprise, he found Stoneridge. "I don't always carry it with me, just in case the Empire gets a hold of me, but I figured that, on this trip…"

Aidan's fingers traced the narrow passages and faint trails marked on the map. He motioned for Mikael. "Come, aye? And hold." He held out his hand. Mikael looked at the bare hand dubiously before glancing back at Katjin. Katjin nodded with a shrug. So, gripping Katjin's hand in one, Mikael took Aidan's in his other.

"Just don't fry me this time," he muttered.

Again, that white hot burst of light jolted through his system. This time, it wound itself around the aiding song that sang through Mikael's mind. The beat of the aiding song seemed to push the shock back, taming it until it was manageable. It still burnt, but Mikael could at least ignore it.

And then, without warning, a flash of fear shot along the burn, followed by the same anger and bile-tasting bitterness that he remembered from his own captivity in the cavalry camp. The fear was very young, while the anger felt older, more resigned. The young fear fought him like a nari cat, growling and scratching, while the old anger seemed to have accepted its fate.

"The marker, Apa!" he heard a voice say. He could feel the mountains, rough under his fingertips, and the flatter peaks of the Highlands. The scrubby grasslands itched at his hands until he found a wide swatch of water to soothe them. The water current carried him down and down, until there was a velvety pocket of grass hidden in the tussock. Stony ridges surrounded him, the feeling so familiar—

"Stoneridge!" he gasped, suddenly thrown out of the light. Katjin's arms were around him, steadying his reeling body. "The cavalry has them near Stoneridge."

They were curled up, alone in the yer. Mikael could hear the faint sound of chatter from the adults outside, but he really didn't care about their grand plan right now. The cavalry had them at Stoneridge, probably within several days' ride of the country house.

And he wasn't going back.

"They might have Mother and Father," he muttered, trying to roll out of Katjin's arms. Katjin's grip tightened around him, not letting him go. "Why else would they be in Stoneridge? Only a bunch of sheep farmers live their. The land's not even good enough for cows."

"Maybe because they think you won't look there," Katjin said softly.

"Or because it's a trap for us," Mikael countered, turning over to face Katjin. His bonded's expression was bleak.

"They don't even know we're still alive," Katjin pointed out. "Their 'paths can't reach this far into the Highlands."

"But they've been here before. They came through on their merry way to get us just moons ago," Mikael reminded Katjin.

"Aye, they did." Katjin was quiet. "Will you do it?"

Mikael lay flat on his back, staring up at the roof of the yer. "What choice do I have?" His voice cracked. Somehow, that choice seemed like it had been made almost before he was born.

The camp located, Soren and Aidan were to be dispatched. There had been debate over whether or not to dye Aidan's bright red hair, since so few in the Empire could boast of hair that shade. At least, tightly braided back as it was in traditional Shahi-style, it could be covered by a hat.

"Leave it," was Soren's final word. "Could be an advantage, if he needs to spring me from a trap or something."

Apa seemed to agree with that, but still insisted on Aidan wearing the same kind of peaked cap that had covered Mikael's head for moons now. "Keep the sun off of you," Apa said, pointing to Aidan's skin that rivaled only Mikael's in paleness. "No one will mistake you for Clan, but you could pass for Highlandfolk, since most Lowlanders have never seen one of them anyway."

Aidan snorted at that. He also refused to wear a Clan robe. "Not Shahi," he pronounced with the same haughty attitude that Katjin and Soren both gave to their own Clan robes. He did concede to wearing Highlandfolk style full trousers under a Lowland-style shirt and his leather jerkin. The soft weave of the fabric fascinated him, and he could be found idly stroking the sleeve of his shirt on occasion.

"A little odd, aye?" Soren remarked as the three of them watched Aidan from across the camp. "I never thought a Shahi demon would be puzzled by linen, of all things."

"Tai said something about them not having any," Katjin said. "They could get wool from the wild sheep that ran through the old City farms, but they didn't have the right kind of flax plants to spin linen."

Mikael fingered the heavier wool robe that he now wore, since temperatures were rapidly falling as they came closer and closer to winter. "Wonder when we'll see snow fall." He was the only one still wearing those woolen and rabbit's fur underthings from Tai, but he wasn't complaining about the cold either the same way Soren and Katjin occasionally did.

Katjin shivered. "No snow, please. I had enough of it in the pass." He turned to Soren with a half-grin. "Can you imagine, telling the cousins about it? About the Shahi, the Highlandfolk..."

"The fact that we're now wanted by the entire Empire and there's probably prices on our heads," Soren reminded Katjin, throwing an arm around Kat's neck and rubbing his knuckles into Katjin's dark hair, messing the two tails up.

"Hey!" Katjin knocked Soren's hands away. "No one said you had to come rescue us from the cavalry."

Soren snorted. "The armed soldiers chasing after you probably begged to differ." The look on his face darkened. "You'll do the same for me, aye? If... if something happens?"

Katjin was startled. Starless hells, Mikael was too, but probably not as much as Katjin. Soren had never admitted to any weakness, nor to any possible danger in anything.

The fact that he was doing it now was a little scary, in more ways than one.

Mikael held out his bare hand to Soren, palm up in the same gesture Aidan often used. Soren put his hand against Mik's, curling his longer fingers over Mikael's. Katjin came up on the other side and did the same thing, til they were linked in a circle.

"We're in this together," Mikael said. "No matter what happens, no matter whose fault—" Katjin grunted at that, but Mikael just glared at him. "Together. We're coming out of this together. All three of us."

"Four, since we have to apparently count Aidan now," Katjin said sourly, nodding toward Mikael's backside. "Your admirer is here."

Mikael looked over his shoulder, not entirely surprised to find Aidan there, looking lonely. "You're just mad that even a Shahi's taller than you," he snapped. "Can't you get it through your thick head that he means nothing to me? It's not like I want to jump into bed with him and Soren and you in a giant foursome."

Katjin's head was bowed, his eyes focused on the ground. Mikael could see the tips of his ears reddening, but his bonded said nothing. Soren, though…

Soren laughed. Dropped their hands and fell to the ground, laughing so hard that he wheezed. Aidan rushed over, looking concerned. "Soren chokes, aye?" he asked, hands knotted up together. "We help, aye?"

Mikael snorted before bursting out laughing himself. "He's fine, Aidan. He'll survive." He grinned at the Shahi, who smiled hesitantly back. "You ready?"

Aidan nodded, yellow eyes serious. "Ready, aye. Mandric says we ride now."

To Soren's dismay, he'd been left out of the final

planning stages. Mandric said it was necessary, because the Empire would most likely use its 'paths to glean whatever they could from Soren's mind. Which prompted Katjin to make a comment about the state of Soren's mind, and then Apa had to wade into the fracas to separate the two of them. For some reason, Katjin was becoming more and more agitated when it came to Soren over the past few days. Maybe it was a sense of impending doom. Maybe Katjin was actually starting to admire his cousin. Mikael didn't want to read too much into it, since it was just one more thing he'd have to deal with.

In any case, the plan was simple enough; Soren would sacrifice himself as bait, hope that the cavalry didn't kill him before Aidan had the chance to signal the others, and they'd ride in to his rescue, hopefully finding what was left of Redwind clan in the process. While it seemed a bit foolish and dangerous to Mikael, he wasn't going to argue with seasoned warriors and men grown, not when he knew nothing of tactics. Soren at least made the promise to fight them hard, when he was captured. All that training at the hands of the Shahi scouts shouldn't go to naught.

Their goodbyes were brief. A quick, hard embrace to both Mikael and Katjin, a muttered "Ancestors bless," and Soren was off. Aidan followed at a more sedate pace, walking, since he still wasn't entirely comfortable on a horse—or with horses, but that was another story.

Coming down from the Highlands into what was traditionally Lowlander territory sparked some tension within the camp. Mandric and Apa had about thirty others with them, a mix of Shahi, Highlandfolk and Clanfolk. Mikael was sure he was the only Lowlander. Aidan, at least, wasn't seen as too much of a surprise or a threat, even if he was the only full, magically-active Shahi.

"Too bad we couldn't fix some horns to his forehead, or convince him to wear a cloak," Katjin said as they watched Soren and Aidan disappear over the horizon. "Might as well take advantage of that whole Shahi demon thing."

Mikael gave Katjin a quick smile. "Are we okay now?" he asked suddenly, not sure where the question came from. "You know that Aidan means nothing more than Soren means, right? They're family, but they're not..."

Katjin nodded. "I know. I just..." He sighed. "You feel out of sorts, aye? You have ever since we went to the Shahi. It's like... we're not in sync anymore."

"Something a little off?" He stretched out his arms, not surprised to see Katjin mimicking his movement. They'd been doing a lot of that—stretching the bond, moving in unison, though one of them always seemed to be a slight step behind.

"Maybe..." Katjin swallowed. "Maybe we're rejecting the bond?" Mikael couldn't ignore the hesitation, couldn't deny the doubt, couldn't excuse the fear he felt coming off of Katjin.

Neither of them had accepted it at first. They'd both fought it tooth and nail. Katjin had even screeched in everloving glory about how he wanted his life back. Mikael wondered when their roles flipped, when he became tired of being the dependent one. Maybe because Katjin had been so strong, and he was tired of being so weak.

"I can shield you, the way you shield me," he said slowly. "You're not the strongest part anymore. I can't *let* you be the strongest part," he corrected, avoiding Katjin's eyes. "I think... I think we need to be equal, for this to work." He looked up. "You protect me. I protect you."

"But—" Katjin's mouth hung open. "We do. We are equal. Don't you feel it?" His hand hovered over Mikael's, not touching, but just enough so that Mikael could feel the body warmth and the low pulse that he associated with the bond.

"Do you recognize me as an equal?" Mikael persisted. "If we're going to do this together, if we're going to stay like this—"

"Don't you want it?" Katjin broke in. "Don't you want to belong to something, to have a purpose? I—"

Mikael caught Katjin's hand in his, turning the calloused palm over and lightly tracing the lines on Katjin's hand. Life line, heart line, head line, fate line: they were all there. "I don't want to belong to something for what I am, but because of who I am," Mikael said slowly. "We can't get rid of the bond—we won't get rid of it, seeing what it did to Aidan. But we have to fix us before the bond works properly."

"Fix it how?" Katjin asked, cross now. He pried his hand out of Mikael's.

Mikael sighed. "Fix it by acting like adults and treating each other like adults. Not second-guessing each other anymore. *Trusting* each other."

Katjin opened his mouth to say something, but then closed it. Then he dropped his eyes again, ashamed. "I'm sorry."

"So you trust me then, about Aidan?" Mikael couldn't help asking, pulling Katjin close again. "Damn it, Kat, it's not like I could sneak off with Aidan without you knowing."

Katjin submitted to the embrace, leaning limply against Mikael. He snorted. "No, I guess not. I just... I feel sorry for him, and I don't want to. He's Shahi! He's a—" He stopped, as if finally noticing Mikael's glare. "I know that's the Empire talking. I know that they're our real enemy, and that they were the ones who put a lot of this into place. But it's hard, aye? It's hard not to protect you, not to pigeonhole you into that one little box that you fit in. I'm responsible for you because you sang the aiding song to me."

Which was probably the simplest the answer.

People of the golden plains
Pleas heard in every breath
Heed our elders, heed our young
Help the family in its need

He sang softly, pushing Katjin's face up so that Katjin couldn't help but meet his eyes. Katjin fought a little bit, but gradually submitted, looking as if he was finally listening to the words of the aiding song.

Each to each and hand to hand
Easing pain and stopping grief
Whose this day can I abate?
Which wish can I help relieve?

And with a slight smile, Katjin sang the same response that Mikael had sung so long ago, sealing their fate.

Me, is mine, I seek relief
My pain is nigh, my heart's hurt
A favor paid, a deed done
Deliver, ease, help this day

Heart song. That's what it was all about. One heartbeat, one fate, one life between them. For better or for worse, for good or for ill, it was his lot now, and he accepted it. It would be harder than anything he'd ever faced, but it wasn't like he had to face it alone.

Mikael took Katjin's hand, leading him back toward the yer that was now theirs and theirs alone.

I will, aye, I will, aye, he sang softly. *Just point me the way.*

Chapter Nine

Shanti and Marae moved in unison, Marae carefully shadowing Shanti's every move. Mikael hung on, knowing that his grip on Marae's saddle and the strap around his waist were all that kept him on Marae's back. He looked to Katjin, who was similarly strapped to Shanti. Apa was taking no chances this time, not with so much at stake.

"Ready, lads?" Apa asked in a quiet voice.

Mikael nodded. "Ready."

One last hand squeeze for Katjin, and Mikael cast himself deep down before spreading *out*. Katjin effectively blocked the extraneous emotions, letting Mikael focus on exactly what he was looking for—Aidan's magical signature and that sense of intense glee that always seemed to accompany it.

He found it, burning white hot to the point of pain. This time, instead of diving right it, he held the lightning at bay, watching it from a safe distance. It spiraled across the landscape, obvious even to Mikael's non-magical eyes.

"Found him," he muttered to Katjin, struggling to keep the fire at arm's length. "We go."

They rode. Mikael didn't know how far or where they went. He followed Aidan's fiery trail, letting Katjin steer the horses to get there. The white-hot light burned more and more the closer they got, but he didn't care. Whatever he couldn't handle, he pushed the excess off on Katjin until his bonded glowed with the same fierce light.

But as they got closer and closer, all he could see was the light. It burned—starless hells, but it burned!—but he clung to the thought of Katjin and wouldn't let himself get sucked into it. He could feel Aidan on the other end, at the same time calling Mikael to him, but at the same time pushing him back, telling Mik to ignore the siren song. The fire flickered around him, welcoming him and promising him cleansing and purity. It caressed him just as Katjin's fingers had last night, touching and sharing the same heat. Mikael grabbed onto that memory and clung to it for all he was worth. He had the fire that he needed, the drive and the searing heat. He could rise to great heights on his own, without the temptation of the magic.

The fire subsided, subdued a little until it was the same fast-flowing current he'd followed just days before. Now, it was as controllable as any other emotion. Now—

"Mik!"

His eyes flew open and he gasped, inhaling deep. White fire still burned around the edges of the landscape, highlighting the familiar rocky ground and forested slopes that slid down toward the Lowlands, and home.

"You didn't say there'd be trees," Katjin said with a crooked smile. Those green eyes were worried.

"What did trees ever do to you?" Mikael coughed out in response. "Where—"

Katjin pointed down the ridge, to a valley that Mikael

knew all too well. The country house sat in that valley.

The stone room, walls still pockmarked and scarred by Mikael's bloody fists, lay under the foundations of the country house.

He closed his eyes, feeling that rush of energy from Aidan fade away. It was replaced soon enough by the ghosts of old memories: childish laughter turned to childish screams, happiness superceded by fear and rage, the sense of protection broken by the inevitability of imprisonment.

"That's my house," he said dully. "They've got them in my house."

Next to him, Katjin shuddered. "The walls," he muttered. "It'll drive the kids crazy. And Meke and Febe—" He looked to Apa. "We can't go in there. Mik can't."

Mikael shook his head. "We're going, Kat. We have to."

"How many do you sense, lad?" Mandric asked. He, at least, seemed apologetic about it.

He tried to push back any emotions that he could, letting Katjin's forced calm surround him. "Soren. Maybe five or ten cavalry. Maybe a full arban at the most."

He could hear the pride in Apa's voice. "And 'paths?"

Mikael pushed himself deeper, trying to separate the hazy wall that seemed to surround the west wing of the country house, where his sisters had their rooms. "Too hard to tell. They're shielded."

"And others?" Katjin's voice shook. "Any others?"

That tangle of subdued anger and fear was obvious enough. It tasted of bile and dark and immature rage, not sure who they should be mad at or why, but knowing that they hated bitterly. "Younglings. Not sure how many, but they're in the ballroom."

Katjin snorted. "Ballroom?"

Mikael opened his eyes, flashing Katjin a quick grin. "Take it up with my sisters," he said. "If they're alive."

"They here?" Katjin squeezed Mikael's hand.

Mik shook his head. "I can't tell. We're too—" He swallowed. "Too far away."

"And Soren?" Apa asked. "How's the lad?"

Mikael grinned for real this time. "Mad. Spitting mad, though more at himself than anyone else. There's some kind of guilt, as if he was distracted by something."

"Probably his own ego," Katjin muttered, though he did look a little nervous.

Mikael elbowed his bound. "I dunno what happened, but it feels like it didn't go according to his plan. So he's angry. And probably wondering why no one's sprung him yet." He probed deeper. "He's in pain, so they've probably beat him pretty good. Nothing that won't heal in the long-run, but some bruises and his head hurts. Maybe they snuck up on him or something while he was taking a piss and not paying attention. In any case, he's alive and pissed off."

Apa laughed. "That's a good sign." He turned to Mandric. "Your men ready?"

Mandric nodded. "As long as Aidan gets his distraction off, and the lads take out the 'paths, we should be okay." He turned to Mikael and Katjin. "You're sure you'll just affect the 'paths this time?" Not that the Empire would be any kinder if they left no casualties, but it was something that none of them wanted on their consciences, especially not with the inevitable war ahead.

Mikael exchanged a look with Katjin, grateful for the

unconditional support he found there. "Aye, we can," he said.

With a quick clasp to each of their shoulders, Mandric pushed them gently toward the path that led down into the valley. "It's time, lads."

They slunk down the path on horseback. It was the same as Mikael had remembered from just moons ago, when he spent any time he could exploring the valley around the country house. This path led down through the woods and almost right up to the servants' quarters. Mikael had done his best to sketch out a map of the house and grounds for Mandric and the others before Soren and Aidan left, so they all knew more or less where they were going. He didn't think they'd changed the house at all in the days of his captivity, but he couldn't be too sure.

Katjin twitched a little bit as they rode deeper into the woods. This time, he rode behind Katjin on Shanti with Marae following docilely behind, since they couldn't ride abreast down the twisting, narrow path. All they needed was to either alert the guards that they were coming, or get injured before they even reached the house. Mandric had protested enough against the use of horses, period, but neither Apa nor Katjin wanted a repeat of last time.

What he would've given for a horse on his last flight out of here.

He tried his hardest not to stray too far back into his memories. All he wanted was to rest his head against Katjin's shoulder and close his eyes, but he had to stay focused, to keep his mind alert. There was always the possibility that they wouldn't make it out of this, and he didn't really want to start thinking about a life alone at this moment. Not now.

Katjin hummed under his breath, something that

Mikael recognized as one of Tai's song-lines. Though it didn't produce any kind of magical result, Mikael could feel the soft tune calming his nerves. He was poised and ready to strike when the moment came, and not a moment before.

It was too quiet in the woods. He almost expected a nari cat to charge out of the underbrush at them, and would almost have welcomed that odd, shrieking cry of the moah. But no birds sang in the woods, and he couldn't even hear the rustling of deer or other hoofed animals in the woods. The mere thought of that automatically raised his anxiety level, but he couldn't let himself get distracted by it. If they were walking into a trap...

"Trap?" Katjin asked quietly, tensing as the spillover emotions hit him.

Mikael brushed his mouth against Katjin's ear. "I think so," he muttered. "I don't know if they realize it's us, though." His hair was completely blond again now, lightened by the constant sun on the plains. What he had of a tan had persisted, even after a moon and more in the Shahi forests. With their wardrobe being an odd mix of Highlandfolk and Clanfolk, they could've been anyone.

Except that it wasn't just anyone who knew this track down into this valley.

"We're Highlandfolk, if anyone asks," Mikael said quietly.

It was almost unnoticeable, but he caught Katjin's nod in response.

They made it within sight of the house. Mikael did his best not to tense up, trying to keep his body as relaxed as possible. They wanted to appear casual, just in case something happened. While they were pretty much guaranteed that they'd reach a guard even before they got to the kitchen gardens, Mikael thought that taking that guard out was within their abilities.

They were a little bit more...*subtle* about it now.

"Wait," Katjin hissed, holding up his hand. "I have an idea." He slid off Shanti, motioning for Mikael to do the same.

Mikael groaned as he dismounted. Katjin's ideas, while creative, weren't always the most well-planned. Or achievable.

"Remember the cavalry?" Katjin continued, head bent close to Mikael's. Before Mikael could say anything, Katjin pressed on. "Not with the sickness, though. What if you send them peace? Make them sleep?"

Mikael considered it. It would be a lot easier on him, as long as he maintained the calm he'd need to project. "We can try it," he said, still doubtful.

Katjin beamed at him, kissing him fiercely. Heat pooled in Mik's stomach and groin. He wanted to swallow Katjin whole, keeping him safe forever. "Starless hells, Kat, don't start that here!"

With a smirk, Katjin kissed him again, quickly this time. "It was to calm you down." He had that innocent look on his face.

Mikael snorted. "Right." He took a deep breath, trying to center himself the way Tai taught. In with the good air, out with the bad. Leaning his forehead against Katjin's, he imagined the old house: the hallways he'd run down as a child, the rooms he'd played in, the dark cellar where—

"Easy, love." A snatch of song, a kiss to his forehead. "In and out. Breathe."

He could almost hear the echoes of his sisters' voices, nagging and laughing at the same time. Mother's soft songs haunted him from around corners, and he swore he smelled her perfume.

His eyelids felt heavy, his limbs weighted down. He pushed this slack of body and mind at the house, relieved as the feeling left him.

"Ancestors," Katjin groaned, straightening up from his slump. "That even made me tired."

Mikael brushed his lips over Katjin's. "We can sleep later. Now…"

Katjin nodded. "Now."

They crept up to the first wall. A guard leaned against the gate, bow lightly gripped in his left hand. An arrow lay across his lap, as if he'd fallen asleep where he stood.

"One down," Katjin said quietly as they moved toward the kitchen garden, leading the horses now. At intervals along the inside of the garden wall, more soldiers slept. Mikael counted four now.

"Should we tie them up?" Mik asked, "Keep them from following us?"

Katjin nodded.

Once the soldiers were trussed and tied, Mikael actually took a moment to look more closely at the kitchen garden.

"So, this is your home?" Katjin asked in a soft voice.

Mikael nodded, trying to ignore the signs of decay and disorder among what had once been orderly rose of vegetables and herbs. "Should we leave the horses here?"

Katjin surveyed the walls. "Are there any other ways out of here?" he asked.

Mikael pointed toward the side gate, a low wooden affair that wasn't much more than decoration. "Leads out to the orchards, and then back to the forest."

Turning to Shanti, Katjin took a hold of her head and whispered something in her ear. The horse whickered at him, as if she understood exactly what he was saying. Knowing Clan horses, it was entirely possible.

"Kat," he said softly, tugging on Katjin's arm. "We have to move now."

His bonded nodded. "Let's go."

They paused before the kitchen door. Mikael couldn't sense anyone within, so they pressed ahead. He was surprised that his sleep had passed this far into the house. He knew better than to press his luck, though.

A twinge of pain shot through Mikael as they moved into the kitchen. The door leaned on its hinges in disrepair, and Cook's beloved kitchen was in shambles. Cupboards half-hung on the wall, broken crockery covering the bench and table. He could hear mice scurrying about in the dark corners, and there was a horrid smell coming from the pantry off to the left. He didn't even want to think about what cold storage was like. Another soldier, obviously in the middle of cooking something, was face-down in a pot of what looked like some kind of stew. Mikael gently turned the soldier's face to the side, so that he wouldn't drown in the soup, while Katjin tied the man's wrists and ankles together.

"Thank the ancestors that we brought that rope," Katjin muttered as they pressed on.

They moved quickly down the servant's hallway and into a passage that led down to the laundry. Not many people actually knew the passage existed, since it cut off from the linen closet next to the servant's privy. The air was musty in the narrow passage, and Mikael had to remind himself to breathe slow and deep, just to keep Katjin from panicking.

"Think of the light," he muttered as they hurried through the passage.

Once they reached the laundry, Mikael stopped again to try and see if he could find Soren. Katjin's cousin wasn't far away; his fury was so obvious that Katjin actually grinned. "Someone's still not too happy. I think you're right. I think they did catch him with his arse in the air —"

The door opened so suddenly that Mikael squawked. He automatically focused a wave of anger at the figure, who actually...dodged.

"Shite!" Katjin grabbed a broom, tossing a mop to Mikael. "Quick!"

As they rushed toward the figure, the figure waved his hand and stopped them.

"Aidan!"

The figure blinked and took off his hat. His snake-like red braid fell to his shoulders, yellow eyes staring at them. "Kat and Mik, aye!" Aidan's face broke into a wide grin. "We distract now." He put his hat back on, stuffing his hair carefully up into it.

Mikael nodded, sighing in relief. "We distract, we find the others, we get out of here."

"Small ones with the large room and Soren," Aidan said, pushing them toward the door.

"And the older ones? My meke and febe?" Katjin asked in a rush. "Where—"

Aidan shook his head, looking a little lost. "No olders, just kids."

Katjin swore softly. Mikael punched him lightly in the shoulder. "We'll find them," he said softly before following Aidan toward the door. "Have you set off the signal yet?"

Aidan shook his head as they made their way down the hallway. "Not yet. Waiting, aye? For you."

"Well, if you wait til we're nearer the ballroom—the large room," Mikael said as they rounded the corner.

Straight into a familiar, but still very tall and looming Lowlander.

"How did you get in here?"

Before Mikael could react, Aidan shot a ball of fire at the figure that stood in front of them.

"Wait!" Mikael said, knocking the man to the floor. "Aidan, this is our seneschal. He's on our side!" He'd been seneschal at the house for as long as Mikael could remember—some old connection to his father's through trade. Mikael wasn't exactly sure on the story, just that Stephan had always been there, at Father's side.

"Mik—"

"Master Mikael?" the older man said, staring up at Mikael as if he was a ghost. "We were told you were dead."

Mikael barked out a quick laugh. "I think Father wished I was," he said, switching into Lowlander.

"Master Mikael!" Stephan the seneschal reproved. "Your father has done everything he could to help you."

Rolling off Stephan, Mikael got to his feet. Stephan stood as well, looking Mikael over with a careful eye.

"Is he all right?" Mikael asked in a rush. "Is Father—"

Stephan nodded, gripping Mikael by one arm and dragging him toward the door. "This way, young Mikael."

Shrugging at Katjin, Mikael had no choice but to follow old Stephan. The halls were quiet as they moved quickly toward the center of the house. He tried to sense if anyone, especially 'paths, were close by, but was having a hard time reading anyone close by but Stephan and Katjin. Even Soren's annoyance seemed to be blocked out somehow.

"Where did you hide?" Mikael asked, panting, as they rushed along. "I found no one here when I—"

"When you ran off?" Stephan's grip on Mikael's arm tightened. "We'd gone away for the day, was festival time, so your father had us all in Stoneridge."

Mikael stopped dead in his tracks. "Everyone, even the servants?" There had been close to ten servants who helped out at the country house. That everyone should be taken into town that day, leaving him behind, seemed highly suspicious

Stephan's eyes narrowed with impatience. "Aye, Master Mikael," the seneschal said, teeth gritted. "Everyone."

Mikael yanked his arm out of Stephan's, a chill running down his spine. "And they left me behind."

"No disrespect meant, Master Mikael, but we were told you'd gone off to recover from your sickness." The emphasis on 'sickness' was all but hissed.

Being trapped in that narrow hallway suddenly seemed like a bad idea.

"Kat, run!" he screamed, heading back the way they came. "We have to—"

He smacked right into a guard, this one blocking their escape route.

"Escape?" Katjin muttered. "Why do I feel like we've been here before?"

"Careful, the one in the hat had a torch," Stephan said, rubbing at his arm. "And the blond is the 'path."

The guard looked down at him in distaste. "Renegade," he snarled, so that Mikael could see his decaying teeth.

"Should we take 'em to the Master?"

Stephan nodded. "He's expecting them anyway."

This time, they were hauled bodily off in the direction of the old ballroom. The guard all but kicked down the door, throwing them in the room. The curtains had all been torn off the walls, and the long windows boarded up. Mikael's heart sank. There went thought of that as an escape route, unless Aidan could set fire to the boards.

As he looked around the dimly-lit room, he realized they weren't alone. A dozen children, little ones on up to his and Katjin's ages, seemed to be clustered around the room. Some of the kids looked up as they walked in, their stoic Clan faces showing no signs of emotion. Mikael noticed that the older ten, boys and girls alike, were all tied together in a long line. At the head of the line was Soren.

Katjin swore under his breath. Soren looked up and groaned. "Damn it, Kat, can't you do anything right?"

"Well, if you hadn't gotten caught in the first place..." Katjin snapped back. The exchange sounded forced to Mikael's ears, after all these moons, though the annoyance rang true. "At least tell me they hit you over the head when you were pissing or something."

To Mikael's surprise, Soren blushed. O-ho, the great warrior that no one could sneak up on, felled while he was relieving himself...

"If you hadn't brought home a blasted 'path, then we wouldn't be in this mess," Soren countered, almost calmly. "First a 'path, then Highlandfolk. Who next, Shahi?"

"Shut up!" A guard cuffed Soren across the face. "Berate your idiot cousin later. For now—"

"For now," a new voice said, one Mikael almost recognized. "For now, we deal with the boys who so thoughtfully delivered our prize."

Chapter Ten

They were separated. Katjin was tied to Soren, and Mikael was bound to Aidan three strides away. He could feel the tugging at the bond, but tried to ignore the pain. There were worse things to think about right now, more serious situations they had to deal with. The damned bond could wait.

The 'Master' looked familiar to Mikael, but he couldn't place the face. It was probably one of Father's business associates, though Father hadn't brought many of them to the country house. The few excursions Mikael had accompanied Father on had always been to Stoneridge, and Stoneridge didn't exactly rate the most sought-after merchants and goods, much to Mikael's sisters' dismay.

Mikael tried to probe the so-called Master, but the Master didn't feel out of the ordinary in any way. The three 'paths the cavalry had used to track him moons ago had almost radiated a kind of power that made their skin crawl. This man, though, didn't feel like a 'path, not that that said a whole lot, in light of Mik's vast experience with thought-senses.

The Master turned to look at him, as if sensing Mikael's scrutiny. "You recognize me, boy?" he asked in a haughty

Heart Song

voice.

Mikael tried to place the graying yellow hair and brown eyes, but nothing was clicking. "No, should I?" he asked through gritted teeth, determined not to let this bastard get the best of him. "Where's my father? Maybe he could remind me."

The Master shrugged. "If you can figure out how to raise the dead, you can ask him yourself."

Hissing in sharply, Mikael looked over at Katjin. He could just barely hear the soft humming, something that Aidan had picked up and relayed to him. It wasn't the aiding song, this time. It was that old martial air that Mikael had sung so often as a child.

Soren called out something to Aidan in Shahi, who fired an answer back. That didn't please the Master, who reached out to smack Aidan this time. Mikael heard the crunch of the Master's hand against Aidan's skull. The Shahi boy glared up at the Master. Mikael chuckled softly.

Fire down, Lowland town/Wooden walls to founder, the old words of the song went. Aidan might not be a demon, but he was a firebrand. A lightbringer.

Maybe it was time to get angry again.

"Aidan, remember the moah?" he asked softly. Katjin picked up on it, though, and grinned.

"Bush moah, or nari moah, aye?" Aidan asked just as quietly. Mikael could almost hear the thoughts racing through Aidan's mind.

"Fire down, Lowland town," he sang softly in Clantongue. Aidan's eyes widened, and then he grinned. "Aye, nari moah, Aidan. Aye?"

Aidan looked thoughtful. "Energy's…" Mikael could feel the shrug through the ropes that bound them, shoulder to shoulder.

"Feed him," Katjin hissed. "Like with me. But give it to Aidan."

Even Soren sucked in a breath at that. "Kat," Soren warned. "You can't—"

Mikael shifted to look at Aidan. "Can you? If I give you my energy, like before, with your father?"

A long, slow nod from Aidan. "Aye," he said with finality.

As their discussion went on, Mikael caught the guards looking at them suspiciously. None of them seemed to look Clan or understand Clantongue, which probably meant that rumors of Clan abandonment of this particular outpost or mission or whatever were true.

"Just what are you—" the Master started to say. But before he could do anything, Mikael closed his eyes. He looked deep into every dark thought he'd had over the past six moons. It wasn't just cavalry and Empire, but his family for leaving him behind and Tai hitting him with that damned stick. It was Katjin, for not trusting him, and Soren for being mean. It was the snow that was starting to fall, and how much he just wanted to be warm in a house somewhere, with windows and doors he could open to let light in. It was the bond that wouldn't let him live his own life, ever again. It was his father's death, undeserved as it was—every unnecessary death, from an Empire that was supposed to bring peace.

It was Stephen's betrayal, and Tai's endless circuit of useless exercises, and if he had to be dragged over a mountain pass one more time, he would doubtlessly scream.

He took all this anger, along with every bit of pain and rage Katjin could feed him. He bundled it up, and then *sent* it to Aidan.

And then the boards covering the windows exploded.

"APA!" Katjin screamed, his voice somehow echoing over the roar of flames and popping wood.

This time, the cavalry came. And they were on Mikael's side.

Apa and Mandric jumped through the flames, as if they had been waiting for that exact moment. The doors opening onto the ballroom were flung open, and the room was suddenly full of soldiers and Highlandfolk and Clan teenagers who were anxious to be untied and join the fight. Aidan sang a second spell, and the ropes themselves seemed to melt away.

"This way!" Mikael called, scooping up the small child nearest to him and herding those in front of him away from the fighting. There was a side door that would lead to a servant's corridor. One of the old larders could be barred from the inside. Or, worse came to worse, they could make their way out. If they could get everyone…

Katjin's girl cousins seemed to understand what he was trying to do. They hurried the kids along behind him. The tallest girls remained with the two oldest boys, standing shoulder to shoulder. Apa and Mandric were tossing long knives to the older kids left and right.

Before the emotions could become too much, Mikael did his best to project an aura of calm down the corridor. He led them down two lefts and then a right, finally opening a heavy door. "Here!" he said, waving them into the room.

Once all six of the younger children were inside, the oldest of the girls shooed him away. "Go back to Uncle Nolan," she said in a soft voice, her eyes looking old in her proud face. "We'll take care of this."

He nodded, then looked to Katjin. Katjin handed his knife to his cousin, pressing a quick kiss to her hand. "Take care of them, Anida," he said, turning back to Mikael. "Ready?"

Mikael grinned. "Aye."

They raced back toward the ballroom, not surprised to find things in shambles. Mandric and Apa and the others seemed to have cornered the soldiers into one corner, while Aidan and Soren battled it out with the man they called Master. As a soldier snuck up on Soren from behind, Katjin ran into the fray, grabbing the nearest shattered table leg. Mikael picked up a leg off the same splintered table.

"Soren! Watch out!"

Soren whirled around, ducking a strike from the soldier. The soldier drew a sword. Katjin's feckless cousin only grinned at the man.

"Is that the best you've got?" So Soren drew his own long knife, pressing in to attack. "That's for sneaking up on me, you bastard!"

One opponent down, the Master stepped closer to engage Aidan in hand-to-hand combat.

"How did you get the Shahi involved?" the Master hissed, catching sight of Mikael. "Demonspawn!" There was a buzzing in his brain, as if his head were full of bees. Only 'paths could cause that kind of sensation, and the Master was no—

"'Path?"

The Master sneered. "Too small to catch your notice, and most other 'paths. The Empire counted on that." Small as it was, it was still annoying the starless hells out of Mikael. He forced himself to concentrate, if only to make the buzzing stop.

Arms raised, the Master held his sword up, obviously about to strike down on Aidan. "Send you back to the starless hells," the Master growled as the sword came down.

Mikael jumped between Aidan and the Master's sword stroke, parrying the swing of the sword with the length of table leg. The sword gouged a deep cut in the wooden leg. "At least the demonspawn are willing to help." His eyes focused on the Master's arms and shoulders, trying to predict where he would strike next. Focusing helped, especially since the buzzing in his head only seemed to get stronger, the closer Mikael got to the Master. He started humming under his breath to take his mind off the buzzing.

And then noticed Katjin creeping up behind the Master, taking up a mirror-image stance behind the Master. A drum began to beat in Mikael's head, and he could hear Tai's voice calling out. His heartbeat echoed the rhythm until Mikael could almost feel the power pulsing within him.

Shoulder. Raising his staff to shoulder-height, Mikael fended off another blow from the Master. The Master was quick; he seemed to anticipate their moves somehow. The anger built, the energy crackling in his bones.

Head. Katjin's table leg lifted to head height, towering just over the Master's. The Master dodged. Concentrating hard, Mikael tried to force as much of that rage into a ball, just as Tai had said.

Parry. The Master swung his sword in an overhand arc. Mikael danced out of the way, not surprised to see Katjin in step with him. They moved as one.

"Now," Katjin mouthed. So Mikael let loose the ball of anger, and it struck.

The Master dropped his guard and stood there, stunned.

Thrust. Mikael's staff came up, catching the Master in the chin as Katjin brought his down, clouting the Master over the back of the head.

Pivot. As one, they both pivoted on their rear foot, turning away from each other. Completing a full turn, Mikael slashed the tip of his staff in an X, as Katjin brought his down at right angles in a cross motion.

Circle parry. As the Master dropped, their table legs clattered in a circle, finally coming to rest in a point over their heads.

Aidan stared at the two of them before breaking out into a grin.

"See? Unison, aye."

The sounds of battle were fading around them as Mikael slumped against Katjin, drained of any energy he had left. Katjin's arms came around him, holding him tight. Aidan wasted no time, binding the Master with what was left of the rope. "Lives," he pronounced, feeling the massive bumps rising from the back of the Master's head. That meant that Apa and Mandric could at least get some semblance of answers, later.

"Kat! Are you—" Apa slid to a stop, staring down at the Master. He turned the Master over with one foot, then gasped as he got a good look at the face.

"You know him, Apa?" Katjin asked, peering down at the Master's slack-jawed face.

"He was one of the merchant guild for these parts," Apa said finally. He looked up at Mikael and Katjin. "He was the one who introduced me to your grandfather, your ama's father."

Mikael's brain tried to rationalize the connection,

but couldn't. "So he knew about the Shahi somehow? Or who might be involved in them?"

Apa could only shake his head. "I wish I knew, lad. I wish I knew half of what I've dragged you into." He tipped both their faces up, one at a time, as if checking for any damage. "Are you hurt?"

Katjin shook his head. "I think we're just... tired," he said, physically drooping. "Meke and Febe! Did you find them, Apa?"

Another shake of his head. "Unless they're hidden somewhere..." Apa's eyes widened. "The kids. Where are the kids?"

Mikael pointed down the hallway. "Stuck them in the old larder," he said. "The house is a warren of old rooms and tunnels. They probably have—" He stopped. It made perfect sense.

"I know where they are," he said, running toward the kitchen again.

Aidan blasted the cellar door open. Mikael pushed to the front of the pack, shining his torch down into the hole. He tried to call out, but his voice stuck in his throat.

Katjin pushed past. "Meke? Febe?" He turned to Mikael. "You don't have to go in, if you don't want to."

Mikael shook his head. "I do, Kat. I do."

They could hear faint scrabbling sounds. As they pressed forward with the torch, Mikael caught the fetid smell that crept out. Darkest night, that was foul. He wondered how much of it was him, and how much of it the more recent captives.

Katjin moved in deeper with his own torch. "Meke?" he tried again, louder this time. "Febe?"

This time, there was a quiet reply. "Kat?"

Mikael could feel his heart breaking with relief. He grabbed Katjin's arm, preventing his bonded from running into the darkness full-tilt. "Go slowly, Kat," he said, steadying Katjin. "They aren't used to the light. Don't blind them too much."

Katjin gave him a wavering smile. "It's me, Meke." This time, his voice broke. "It's me and Mikael."

"Mikael?" A new voice now, one with a Lowlander accent probably seizing on the only word it knew. "Mikael." The word seemed to bounce off the stone walls, reverberating deep through Mik's body and back out again.

Heart feeling like it was trying to pound its way out of his chest, Mikael made his way into the small room that had imprisoned him for so long.

Aidan muttered something, casting small globes of light about the room. It was smaller than Mikael remembered, barely five strides long and wide and smelled of overflowing pots and human misery. Two older Clanfolk were huddled in the corner closest to the door, both struggling to get to their feet as Katjin collapsed next to them, into their arms. It was the four at the back of the room, though, that interested Mikael.

"Your family," Aidan said slowly. "Mother with sisters, aye?"

Mother, Lina, Mei, Emera. Mikael stared at them, mouth not working despite his attempt to force the words out.

"Mikael?" It was Emera's voice that repeated his name, as she blinked in the faint light of the globes. "But you're just a trick, aren't you?" She sounded resigned, tired, cross. "If they're trying to use Shahi into scaring us now, then I'm done with them."

"Don't be so contrary," Mei hissed to Emera. Mikael had to stifle his laughter. These were his sisters, all right, no Empire trick about it.

"Father. Where's Father?" He moved no closer, not wanting to push the bond further than he should. He was so tired now, and all he needed was to black out again. But he needed to know the truth, if the man that was called Master had killed Father.

"Father's been dead for moons, lured out by a false business deal," Emera said quietly, matter-of-factly. "You know this. Why do you keep asking us?"

Lina and his mother wouldn't say anything, or couldn't. They just held on to each other, rocking and weeping silently.

Mikael looked at Aidan, who nodded. "I fetch Mandric, aye," he said, before racing off. Luckily, the globes didn't follow him out, but hovered in the corners of the small room, as if anchored there.

"Mik?" Katjin's hand touched his elbow. "You need some help?" He nodded toward Meke and Febe, who were shakily standing on their own feet. In the cold light of Aidan's globes, they looked tired and sick, but there was no denying the anger that burned inside them, the drive for blood in exchange for their own losses. "They're all right, for all they've been through. Your folks, though…"

Mikael snorted softly. "Kat, meet my mother," he said in Lowlander, the words feeling funny on his tongue. "And my sisters, Lina, Mei and Emera."

Katjin bowed to them in proper Lowlands style. "A pleasure," he said, as strange as the polite phrasing sounded in this particular situation. "Can we help you up?"

Emera stared at Katjin, and then looked at Mikael. "Mei, he's real."

Mikael reached down to his sister, pulling her up gently. "Aye, Em. I'm real," he said softly, wondering when she'd gotten so small and frail.

Frail as she might appear, her grip on him was so tight that it hurt as she hugged him. He pushed her away gently before the pain began, happy that he'd put his gloves back on before they came down into the bowels of the country house.

"If you're real, why are you dressed like Clanfolk?" Emera asked, her voice sounding clearer now. Mikael kept one arm around her waist, supporting her slight weight.

Katjin snorted, but didn't say anything. Mikael wasn't sure what to do or say, and since his bonded wasn't exactly being helpful... "They answered the aiding song," he finally said, figuring that the simple truth was the easiest one.

Emera's dark eyes—not unlike Kat's, when Mikael thought about it—widened. Then she smiled slightly, pushing some of her limp dark hair out of her eyes. "I never thought that would ever come in handy." Her smile faltered. "Not that it would've worked on the Clanfolk in the cavalry, when the cavalry arrived."

Mei hauled herself to her feet, wobbling unsteadily. "They said you were dead. That you betrayed the Empire." Her voice was almost accusatory, and her eyes kept flicking back and forth between him and Katjin. "You're sure that wasn't a Shahi that first walked in here?" He didn't know whether he should be relieved or dismayed at how clear his sisters sounded. Lina and his mother, though…

"How long has she been like this?" Mikael asked, ignoring Mei for a minute. "Mother and Lina?"

Emera shook her head. "Not since we were dragged back here a moon or so ago. When Mother heard that Father's meeting with the merchant hadn't gone well, she packed the three of us up and headed for Grandmother's, down on the coast. The cavalry caught up with us there about two moons ago."

Mikael gritted his teeth, trying to force back the anger that his family had just left him there, in the dark. He could only imagine what being in this cramped space would be like, filled with furious people, all yelling at each other. "And Father—"

"Dead." His mother's voice was clear. "Dead, just like the rest of us."

"Mik, maybe we should get them out of here," Katjin said quietly, tugging on Mik's free arm. He glanced back at Meke and Febe. "I can call Soren and the others to help your ama and sisters out of here."

Mikael snorted. "You just don't want to be alone with them in this room," he replied back in Clantongue. Never was he so glad that none of his sisters spoke it. He turned back to his family. "Em, can you stay with Mother and Lina? I'll get Mei settled and come back for the rest." Someone else could deal with Mei's petulant whining for a while.

Shifting his grip to Mei and making sure that her bare skin wasn't touching any of his, he helped her toward the door. His mother began keening, and Lina wasn't far behind her.

"Mikael!" Before he could respond to Emera, though, Katjin's Meke went to her.

"I will stay with you," Meke said softly, taking Emera's hands in hers. "Let the boys get help, and we'll be out of her soon enough."

Aidan met them at the door, Soren and Mandric not far behind. "My mother and sisters," Mikael panted in Clantongue, dragging Mei's faltering body toward the stairs and *out*. "Meke and Febe too."

Soren took off at a mad dash, calling for Meke and Febe even before he got to the door, relief and joy streaming behind him. Aidan flashed Mikael a brief smile before following after.

"Good job, lad," was all Mandric said before scooping up Mei and heading back through the hallway with her, into the light.

Katjin's arms came around him, holding him close. Mikael allowed himself to lean into Katjin's body for a moment, breathing deeply.

"Easy," Katjin said, rubbing his hand in circles on Mikael's back. "We got them out. We found them."

Mikael looked up, touched Katjin's face lightly. "Aye," he said. "But what do we do now?"

They got Mikael's family and Meke and Febe settled in the old ballroom with the rest of the children. Katjin's young cousins had all made a mad scramble for their grandparents, wailing and crying and shouting so much that it hurt Mikael's ears. Katjin ran a soothing hand up and down Mik's back, which helped. The relief was overwhelming, even though a stark numbness lay under that terrible joy. Mikael knew that all of them had lost at least one parent, some of them older brothers and sisters

Heart Song

as well.

"Twelve left," Katjin said softly. "Twelve, plus Meke and Febe, out of a camp of twenty-five. And Soren only escaped because Meke and Febe sent him with us." He kicked at the stone wall, a brief flare of rage escaping his tight control. Mikael knew how tightly-strung Kat was now, trying to keep his own feelings reined-in until they had dealt with his clan. "Three aunts, three uncles, and my four oldest cousins."

Mikael couldn't even guess at the pain, and really didn't look forward to sharing a camp with this much grief. Selfish as it might seem, he had his own guilt to deal with. He didn't need the stares of twelve children, half of whom were even old enough to understand his part in the deaths of their families. That was ten more lives on his head. But if he thought about it, then he'd only be dragged as deep as the rest. He needed to be strong, if only to prevent the same outpouring of emotion that seemed to follow his darkest moods and fits of tears.

"No guilt," Katjin said fiercely. "We all had our choices. And if anything, we're going to share this one." He looked thoughtful. "What if we—" Katjin wiggled his fingers. "If it works with the bad feelings, it should work with the good."

Mikael nodded. Hard as he tried, though, he couldn't seem to find the sense of peace and calm to really send them. All he felt was empty, even after finding his family.

So Katjin did that part for him. Warmth and content filled the emptiness until it overflowed. The emotions kept coming and coming, and all Mikael could do was act as a conduit letting them flow out and over into the room.

Apa obviously noticed what they were doing, because he turned to them and gave them a slight smile. Though the constant current of emotion burned a little as it came through him, Mikael was just happy that it was over, that this part was done, and that they could move on to the next step—but maybe after resting for a little while. From the looks on the faces of the children—from the babies on up to the oldest—Mikael had a feeling that they'd gained twelve new allies. Thirteen, actually, if you counted the baby that Mikael hadn't seen before. The Clans were insular, aye, but they took care of their own and asked no help from outsiders. When you brought violence down on one Clanfolk, you brought it down on the whole Clan, and had best be prepared to see the entire body of the Horse Clans riding down on you in vengeance.

Children had no business in war. If Katjin's cousins were anything like Mikael suspected, though, there would be no stopping them, not when it came to regaining their families honor and putting their spirits to rest. Mikael understood that now. It's not a lesson he ever wanted to learn, but now, he knew. The anger was palpable, but it was necessary fuel for his fire, and he knew they had a long way to go before it was over.

Once the crying ceased and tentative smiles appeared on most of the faces, Mikael allowed himself to collapse against the wall. From her place in the corner, Emera was waving frantically at him, but he just didn't feel up to dealing with that, not yet. Not when his sisters had abandoned him so easily.

"Easy," Katjin whispered, rubbing his back again. "Let it all go." Humming softly, he handed Mikael a leather skin. Taking the cap off, Mikael took a large swallow. He coughed.

"Aisrag?" he asked, his mouth on fire. The alcohol slid down his throat, helping to soothe a bit of the burning, relaxing the muscles he hadn't realized were tensed.

Katjin smirked. "Soren thought we could use it." He tugged on Mikael's hand. "C'mon, there's family you need to meet."

Mikael was led into the thick of the knot of people, to where Meke and Febe were enthroned on a pile of pillows and cushions, their grandchildren scattered at their feet. A young woman, maybe Soren's age or a little older, cradled a baby to her chest. He remembered hearing something about a baby being born just as Katjin brought him into camp. He was happy that ama and baby had survived, at least, even if Katjin's aunt looked just as battered and malnourished as the rest of the lot. Her eyes burned, though, with the same fire as the others. One more for the cause.

Meke, a short and round Clanswoman, stood up to her full height as he and Katjin approached. Her mostly-gray hair had been tidied, pulled back into the same two tails that he and Katjin still wore. Her dark eyes, though tired and undeniably sad, gave him an appraising look as he walked toward her.

"They fattened you up," she said in assessment. "You're no longer a walking skeleton. I'm glad that Kat and Soren had that much sense, at least."

He held out his forearm to her, surprised when she grasped it, then pulled him toward her and kissed him gently on the forehead. "There's still some fattening up to do," she said, sniffling a little. He could see tears at the corner of her eyes. "Ancestors bless that I have that chance, at least."

Mikael nodded, not sure of what else to say. Meke saved him that choice, though, turning to Katjin. "And you, little Kat." She snorted in disapproval. "Your hair needs trimming, and I swear, you've taken worse care of your clothes than you did with your apa. Even when the Empire's chasing you—" Her voice broke. "Oh, Katjin." Mikael stepped back a little, letting Katjin hold his meke hard, looking at the wall and trying to blink away some of his own tears. He hummed to himself, trying to keep his own emotions steady. All they needed was to set off the room again, especially since he was still wound tight.

"Mikael, lad." It was Febe's voice, his hand warm on Mikael's arm. "We're proud of you, son. And we're proud to welcome you into our Clan, if you'll have us." Turning around, Mikael could read the sincerity in Katjin's grandfather's eyes. There was regret, too. "If we'd made you Clan in the first place…"

Mikael laughed a little. "It would've been the same result. Just… maybe with one or two less kidnappings." And maybe a few less deaths, but he didn't need to dwell on that now. Nor did the kids need to be reminded.

Febe joined in his laughter, his own voice as rusty-sounding as Mikael's. "I think you're right about that, lad."

Meke finally released Katjin, then smoothed down her wrinkled and dirty robe. "When are we getting out of here? The cavalry will certainly be close, and we don't want to be here when they arrive."

"But it wasn't the cavalry, Meke," Katjin spoke up. "Most of the Clanfolk in the cavalry deserted when they heard what happened to the camp. These were mercenaries the Empire hired from the south."

Meke's eyes widened. "We still have to leave, though," she insisted. "I'm not losing these children again." She spotted Katjin's apa across the room. "Nolan, we must have horses. If we lose them on the plains…"

Apa walked toward them, shaking his head. "We're not going back to the plains, Ama," he said firmly. "We've horses plenty outside, but we're taking you to the Highlands."

"The Highlands?" one of Katjin's younger boy cousins piped up. "But that's close to the Shahi demons, and they'll eat us alive." The boy scowled. "'Cept I'll just beat 'em up, 'cause they're just as bad as the Empire." His hands, young as they were, already gripped the knife he wore at his belt. Mikael didn't want to think about the nightmares that boy would have, night after night, about what happened to his family and what he'd do to those monsters.

Mikael grinned at Aidan, who had managed to keep his peaked cap on his head, red hair still carefully tucked up under it. "The Shahi aren't that bad," he said, including Mandric in his grin. "Long as you stay away from the moah and the nari cats, you're fine, but they're all the way on the other side of the mountains. You'll be all right."

The little boy's eyes widened. He couldn't have been much older than eight or nine. "You met Shahi?" He turned toward Katjin with an accusing look. "Kat, how come you never told us you knew Shahi?"

"Because now you know one too." Katjin gestured to Aidan, pointing to his head. Aidan complied, pulling off his hat and releasing that thick red braid. "See? That's Aidan. He's not a demon, but he's definitely Shahi. And he helped get you out of here."

The little boy's brown eyes grew wider and wider. Aidan walked over to the boy, kneeling and holding out his forearm. The little boy grasped Aidan's arm, wrist to wrist, and shook it. "Thank you," he said, small voice trembling slightly.

"Aye, welcome," Aidan said, grinning cheekily. Then, he turned back to Katjin and Mikael. "We go now, aye? To hills?"

Katjin nodded. "I guess we need to herd everyone out."

It was easy enough to get Katjin's family situated. None of the Clanfolk wanted to be stuck inside that house for longer than they had to, and the younglings moved eagerly enough, once they realized they were free to leave, especially with the new purpose in their steps. They might not have moved quickly, but they were driven, and a force to be reckoned with.

Mikael's family, though, was another matter.

"I'm not leaving my house!" Mei shrieked. She had to be carried out bodily by one of Mandric's men. "If I can't pack a wardrobe, how will I properly represent my family?"

Neither Lina nor his mother seemed to respond to anything, so they had to be carried out by Apa's men and tied on horseback, riding double with a couple of Katjin's older girl cousins. The one riding with Mother, probably about his and Katjin's ages, gave him a shy smile as she talked to his mother in a low voice. At least he knew Mother would be taken care of, even if she didn't know it.

Emera, once she was sitting on one of the mercenaries' stolen horses, seemed to regain some of her color and composure. She watched Mei's antics with a serene eye, all the while avoiding looking at where Lina and their mother sat, off to the side. Katjin knew he wasn't the only one who would carry scars away from this, and that nightmare of a room. She nudged her horse over toward where Mikael was saddling up Marae.

"Picked up a Clan horse?" she asked, the envy clear in her voice. "You're going to tell me the story eventually."

He looked up at her, wondering what he owed her for leaving him behind. The worst of the fever had been gone by then, when the women fled. It wouldn't have been that hard to tie him to a horse the same way Lina and Mother were. The cellar door hadn't been magically sealed in any way, since only Shahi could do that. Would it have been so hard to haul him out of that noxious hole, drug him into oblivion and ride off with him? Katjin and Soren had pulled it off.

"If we have time and once we have you settled," he said noncommittally. He mounted Marae, sighing in relief as Katjin did the same and nudged Shanti closer to Marae. "We leaving soon?" he asked Kat.

"You can't avoid us forever," Emera said, angry now. "Whatever betrayal you think we're guilty of—"

And with all of his strength, and with Katjin all but singing at the top of his lungs to Mikael, Mikael turned his horse and rode away.

"So we'll take the women and children up then," Mandric was saying as Katjin and Mikael rode closer. "It's winter, and the Empire won't dare invade the Highlands til at least spring. Especially since they haven't bothered up to this point."

Apa nodded. "And if worse comes to worse, we take them over the mountains. Tai pointed out a few old Cityfolk settlements not too far out of the pass that we could settle them in come spring."

"If Tai's still speaking to us." Mandric inhaled deep. "I hope it doesn't come to that." He turned toward Mikael and Katjin. "What about you lads? Do you want to go with your meke and febe?"

Katjin looked at Mikael, who shrugged. "Apa, can we stay with you?"

Apa gave them both a long look before smiling at them. "Kat, I'd planned on it."

They rode, but this trip into the Highlands seemed a little easier, a little bit more lighthearted than the last one. It made a big difference, when you didn't have the cavalry behind you. Apa and Mandric sent Katjin's oldest cousins out as runners to all the Clan camps, letting them know exactly what had happened. If one Clan arban had defected, chances were that more had, or would, and no one could track Clanfolk through their own plains, not if they didn't want to be found. If the Empire did that, breaking a pact of generations, even the Lowlands might riot. After all, if the Empire went back on their deal with the Clanfolk, who was to say that they wouldn't take equal action against innocent Lowlanders? No one would stand for that kind of blatant tyranny.

Mikael's mother and Lina were transferred to a litter and carried that way up the steep hill trails. Emera and Mei were able to sit their own horses, though they both tired easily. Though Mikael noticed tired eyes and drooping bodies, Katjin's cousins seemed unfazed by everything they'd been through. As resilient as children and Clanfolk seemed to be, Mikael couldn't help but worry. As consumed by this new desire for vengeance as the younglings seemed to be, even down to the knife-carrying six year old, Mikael hoped it would be enough to carry them through. Clan bonds were strong, but he didn't know if they were that strong.

"No one's a kid for long on the plains," Katjin had said once. Mikael believed it now.

Meke insisted on cooking for the entire army of them, since they were an army now. She was doing her best to fatten up Mikael's family through her frybread, one of the few things that his mother and Lina would actually nibble on, if you put it in their hands.

She also looked at all three of Katjin's sisters, just to make sure there were no after effects to their exile. His mother was lost, Meke said, unable to come back to this world. His sisters, though…

"Your Lina will recover, I think," Meke said that first night back in 'real' camp. "She's still young and flexible, much like our younglings." She smiled slightly. "She's probably just waiting for the right moment to displease her, and then she'll voice her feelings to us all. I wouldn't worry too much, Mikael."

She paused. "Your ama, though, Mikael." Meke shook her head. "She says something about a son, a son lost to the Empire. Do you know anything about that?"

There had been rumors and whisperings of an elder brother, but it was nothing Mikael's family would ever tell him about. When he asked Apa, though, Apa was at least able to shed some light.

"The Empire has apparently suspected your father even longer than they've suspected me," Apa said with a slight grin, when they asked him that night. "According to your seneschal, there was a firstborn boy—a 'path— who was taken by the Empire as a child. The Empire's thought-senses hadn't seen signs of any gifts at birth, but the boy was obviously developing them as an adolescent. So he went to the City."

Mikael sucked in a breath, knowing this couldn't end well. "He died, didn't he?" Mikael wondered if he'd always known about this, and had just never been able to pinpoint the exact story, the exact words.

Apa nodded. "He died. This was before you were even born. Even when they took the boy away, your father fought to the point that he was branded as 'disloyal to the Empire.' The Empire sent Stephen to watch your household, though his connection to the Master…" Apa sighed. "The only connection I can make is that they thought your apa might go to the Shahi the way Katjin's ama's parents did."

It was almost too much to think about, especially since the web seemed to entangle itself the more and more Mikael tried to decipher it.

Mikael and Katjin rode ahead with Mandric each day, to give Mikael the peace he needed. Camp was occasionally too loud for him—phyiscally and emotionally—but they had their own yer to retreat to, set up out where the horses were pastured. There wasn't another yer for strides, giving them the emotional privacy they needed, since not even the stoicism of Horse Clan youth could withstand the nightmares that came. That privacy came in handy for other reasons, Mikael discovered, especially as the nights grew colder and body heat became increasingly more important.

Febe cajoled the kids into a good humor each night, leading them in songs and stories that probably sustained them through their captivity. Tired as they were after long days of being on the move, especially after being captive for so long, they dropped off to sleep almost as soon as they got to camp. Those that still had energy were drilled by Soren and Aidan until they, too, were beyond exhausted. The youngest were still skittish, clinging to Meke and Febe and even Katjin and Apa long after their bedtime. Any member of the older generation seemed to be the only thing that would comfort them.

Katjin's youngest aunt thrived, and baby Layla was the darling of the camp. Even as the temperature dropped and they moved higher and higher into the Highlands, Layla still cooed her way through each day. Aidan in particular was entranced with her, carrying her mile after mile in her sling.

Aidan still refused to ride a horse. With the litters, though, and the kids still recovering physically and mentally, it wasn't too much effort for him to keep up with each day's riding. Mikael supposed that climbing rocks wasn't that much different from climbing trees, especially with no nari cats to chase you.

"So you really lived with the Shahi?" the little ones persisted, asking him and Katjin and Soren for stories over and over again. "You really got chased by a nari cat?"

Soren eyed Katjin at that. "You never told me that one," he said, sounding more than a little put-out.

Katjin grinned. "Didn't I mention the day Aidan almost blew up the nari cat?"

Then twelve pairs of eyes turned toward Aidan, who was quickly becoming a favorite among the kids.

"Aye?" Aidan said, when he noticed the expectant eyes. "I blew up the nari cat. It went…" He made the shape of a blast with his hands.

"He didn't," Mikael cut in, noticing how wide some of those eyes got, especially in light of the nightmares that were starting to haunt him, leaking from the children's dreams until he and Katjin pitched their yer further and further away each night. Now, the accusing eyes turned toward him. "He didn't blow up the nari cat, but he did make the bushes catch on fire and almost burned the cat and the moah he was trying to save."

Even Soren shot looks of admiration at Aidan for that.

"What do you think of our new alliance?" Apa asked the night of the first snow's fall. Soren and Aidan were entertaining the kids once again, while Meke and Febe rocked and comforted as they had to. Even Lina showed a little interest tonight, though it might've just been to whatever sarcastic commentary Emera and Mei were whispering in her ear.

"Is this it?" Katjin asked. "Your great plan?"

Mikael took in the Shahi and the Clansman entertaining the circle of Clan children, some of whom sat in laps both Lowlander and Highlandfolk. Katjin's aunt sat near Mikael's mother, bouncing Layla on her knee, every so often showing Mother the giggling baby. His mother's blue eyes were still vacant, but some of the tension seemed to have left her face.

"It is a great plan," Mikael said slowly, overwhelmed by the feeling of peace within the camp. It might not have been content, but everyone was at least peaceful and complacent. "Look, Kat. Everyone's getting along. No one's fighting about land rights, or who was wronged by who in the past. They're all just…"

"Healing," Apa supplied. "Is that the word you were looking for?"

Mikael nodded. "Healing." He smiled shyly at Apa. "That's your plan, aye? Yours and Tai's and Mandric's? It's to heal, not to break."

"We don't want to break the Empire itself, just its hold,"

Apa said, staring into the fire. "We've been separated and turned on each other, and there was no need for it. While the Empire did unite us in the beginning, I think that its end will be what really brings us together."

"And you needed Mikael to do it?" Katjin asked, sounding puzzled. "Couldn't you use Ama, or any of the other renegade 'paths?"

Even Katjin twitched at the quick wave of regret from Apa. "It was too late for that," he said finally. "It was too late when her mother and father took her to Tai's father to have her gift burnt out. Tai knew we'd need an empath, just because thought-senses don't have the kind of reach that a heart-sense does. And since Mikael's disproved every thought we had about what a heart-sense's limitations are..." He smiled at Mikael.

Mik blushed. "I didn't mean to," he muttered, looking down at his feet. "What now, though?"

"We let the Empire topple itself," Apa said. "We spread rumors, we spread the truth, and we make sure everyone knows exactly what the Empire's capable of. We bring the dissent to the surface, and from there..." He made a pushing motion with his hands. "The house falls."

"And we all get to help," Katjin said, as if he just wanted to hear it again. "Me and Mik, Soren and Aidan..."

Apa laughed. "Little Kat, somehow I don't think we could do it without you."

Epilogue

They stood an arm's length apart, not touching, but knowing. Being. He could feel Katjin, humming with emotion and heart beating to the same rhythm, within touch if he needed it. That's how they were supposed to be—not twins, tangled together so tight that they couldn't breathe, but two halves of the same whole, independent, yet stronger together.

Mikael reached out his hand, taking Katjin's in his. He ran his fingers over the square palm, touching the dirty nails and bruised knuckles. He brought one hand up to his mouth and kissed each bloody knuckle gently.

"We're going to do this," he said quietly. "We're going to do this together, and we're going to work. Our family is safe, and now it's time to make sure everyone else is."

There was always a storm before the sun came out. Even the starless hells had to be engulfed in full dark before they could be brought back into the light. And if the Empire thought it was going to fool one more generation into thinking that it was the savior of all humanity…

…it had another thing coming.

"It's time," Katjin said as they turned their back on the Highlands and headed back to the plains. "It's time."

Heart Song

KL Richardsson

Heart Song

Printed in the United States
148163LV00001B/36/P